A Holiday Reunion

AN AURBOR GROVE INN SHORT STORY

(HAPPILY EVER CHRISTMAS)

LAKESHIA POOLE

LUEMARIE

Contents

Also by Lakeshia Poole

Happily Ever Christmas

Renew: 40 Prayers and Prompts to Power Up Your Life

Faith Beats Fear

Don't Let Me Fall

Exes and O's

Don't Post That: A Guided Journal for Saving Jobs, Peace, Edges and Lives

Follow Lakeshia Poole online:

www.Facebook.com/LakeshiaPooleWrites

www.Twitter.com/JustLakeshia

www.Instagram.com/LakeshiaPoole

Sign Up for FREE chapters, behind-the-scenes, and more:

www.LakeshiaPoole.com

Dedication

And another one for Betty Poole :)

It's a Christmas Reunion, Y'all!

Group Chat: Nell, Ramona, & Jasmine

Nell: Okay, ladies we are T-minus 7 days until Christmas and 5 days out from the reunion. Are we good?

Ramona: We are good on my end.

Jasmine: All good. My job is trying to keep me locked up here, though.

Ramona: FREE my girl J, LOL :)

Nell: Well, if you need anything done, let me know. I'm in town early. Fam wanted to participate in the Jingle Bell Festival.

Ramona: Awww, that will be fun. Let's link up.

Nell: We definitely will. How are we looking on tickets for the reunion?

Ramona: Meh. It's alright. This event MIGHT pay for itself.

Jasmine: That bad, hunh?

Nell: I'm sure it will be fine.

Jasmine: Why did we decide to do a 15-year reunion, again? Nobody does that.

Nell: Some folks didn't make it to our 10-year. Besides it's not like it's a real reunion. Just a one-night thing.

Jasmine: Some folks? Do you mean you?

Nell: I mean...

Jasmine: It's just this is a crazy time. We all have so much going on. I had a work 'emergency' so I had to change my check-in time.

Nell: Oh, man I'm sorry Jazz.

Jasmine: It doesn't look like I'll be able to make it in town until Friday. This reunion is a headache we could have avoided.

Ramona: So everybody's staying at the Aurbor Grove Inn, huh? I'm the only lame who has to stay at her own house.

Nell: We can come stay at your house if you'd prefer that. I know my husband would prefer FREE over what we're spending staying at the Inn.

Ramona: I didn't say all that.

Jasmine: You can sleep on the couch in my room Ramona. I'll only charge you $50.

Ramona: Now that would be bring back memories of me sleeping over at your house. Only thing missing is waking up to the smell of Mrs. Wanda's breakfast, can you hook that up?

Jasmine: You're on your own there.

Nell: I just saw the numbers you sent Ramona. Forty people? I know our class is small, but…that's it?

Jasmine: That's what I mean. All this work for so few people to even sign up to come!

Ramona: It's going to be an intimate gathering. Exclusive. This is a VIP-level type of affair.

Jasmine: Nice way to reframe it, LOL

Nell: Life is precious.

Ramona: That's so true. It's not about the number. It's about the ones who can get together. Some of our classmates aren't here anymore.

Nell: And I'm looking forward to actually seeing ya'll live and in person and not just on my Facebook timeline.

Ramona: Me too.

Jasmine: Love ya'll!

A Divinely Designed Christmas

Nell

December 20, 2016

I tapped lightly on the cream-colored door bearing the room name in a gold script against a black placard: The Rose Room.

"Bella?" I said softly. We'd argued enough, and she'd made it clear that I embarrassed her plenty, so I didn't want to cause another scene.

A few seconds ticked away.

Hands on hips, I wondered what was taking this child so long to open the door. I know she was not still asleep.

"Hey, can you open up?" I knocked again.

I checked my phone — it was 11:04 pm. I called her and the phone went straight to voicemail.

That was strange. I didn't hear any movement. I leaned my ear against the cold door. The TV was on — a comedian told a joke, and the crowd laughed raucously.

My pounding heart and shallow breaths rhythmically came together, drowning out all other noise.

My baby. *What is going on?*

I rushed back to our room next door.

Emery saw the panic on my face. He quickly jumped up from the barely comfortable couch. "What is it?"

"It's Bella. I-she's not answering." I rushed about, frantically searching through our bags for some reason.

I poked my head in the bathroom, then went back into the seating area, where he stood paralyzed. "Where is the extra key to her room?"

He pulled it from his pants pocket and beat me to the room. We could not get in there fast enough.

The belly-laughter pouring from the TV atop a dresser contrasted with our distressed states.

The room had all the signs of Bella — it was as messy as her bedroom at home, but there was no Bella in sight.

My world was spinning. I couldn't breathe. I couldn't think. My child was gone.

What had I done?

36 Hours Ago - December 19, 2016

I wanted to ask my husband Emery to make a U-turn on the interstate. Not because of traffic.

There was plenty of that, but that's not what caused me to consider forsaking the money and time we had already invested in our trip from Washington, D.C. to South Georgia.

It wasn't the tiny car the rental company dumped us with — instead of the SUV we requested—that had me wanting Emery to press the brakes.

It was my 16-year-old daughter Bella Michelle Devereaux-Rogers' mouth.

I shouldn't have been surprised she was throwing a wrench in my plans. We were entering year four of her flexing her independence and attempting to figure out boundaries.

I gave in way more than my Mama ever did with me, but if you let her tell it, I was the strictest mother ever to exist.

I've got to give it to her making her wild request two hours into a four-hour road trip with — this was a smart way to convince your parents to let you have your way.

Here I was, heading home for the first time in a long time when she decided to clue me into her ulterior motives for the trip she begged me to take months ago.

When we were back home in D.C., Bella played on my emotions, listening intently to my Christmas stories of fond memories of attending my hometown's annual Jingle Bell Festival, saying she wished she could go. I'd never considered visiting.

Growing up there and all of the things I went through during my high school years made me want to get as far away as possible. Besides, most of my family members had either passed or moved away from Aurbor Grove, so the good and painful memories were all I had left.

Bella and I both adored all the holiday movies showcasing small towns' charm and Christmas spirit, and part of me wanted her to experience it in real life. To know the beauty and kindness of a place where everybody knows your name.

I had no intention of her witnessing the other side of that, where everybody knows your business and judges every move you make.

It just so happened that my 15-year class reunion was occurring at the same time, so it felt like perfect timing. Instead of me and Emery going down for a couple of days and heading back to D.C. for Christmas, we decided to spend an entire week and Christmas Day down South.

I planned to attend my class reunion, catch up with old friends, and show off my success as the Owner of Divine

Designs, the go-to interior design firm for D.C.'s elite. My motto was if your home didn't feel like heaven, you invested in the wrong interior designer. Homes are to be designed for peace, and comfort, and as a respite from this wild and crazy world.

I'd have my fine, 6'2" former pro-baller-turned-tech startup founder husband, "The" Emery Rogers, on my arm and plenty of pictures of Bella on my phone. I also looked forward to introducing Emery and Bella to my childhood holiday traditions at the Jingle Bell Festival since all we ever did was linked to my husband's D.C. roots.

This was me applying my "Divine Design" principles that I used in my business to my personal life. Life is only as great as you make it to be!

I booked rooms at the Aurbor Grove Inn and reserved tickets to several activities. As I plotted out each detail for our week-long itinerary, I saw the three of us laughing, enjoying hot chocolate, going ice skating, and doing all the Christmas things perfect families do. We were the epitome of beauty and excellence, proof that a little country girl from the middle of nowhere can have it all — an amazing career and family—if she possessed faith and worked hard enough.

You see, I had it all laid out perfectly. We were on our way, joking about how being cooped up in a coup would keep us close. We sang along, poorly, I might add, to "Have Yourself A Merry Little Christmas," then "Jingle Bells," while Emery beat-boxed on the steering wheel.

"Okay, what song should I play next?" I asked.

Then, like a record scratching, my daughter didn't request a song, but a Christmas miracle...

"I want to visit with my Dad's family while I'm in Aurbor Grove."

The confidence, the certainty, the unmitigated gall of my

bold and intelligent daughter — I admired it for three seconds. Then the words echoed in my mind.

"I want to visit with my Dad's family while I'm in Aurbor Grove."

I hadn't seen her father's family since leaving town on a one-way ticket to anywhere but here. This was the 'ugly side' I didn't even want to think about, let alone revisit.

Why couldn't we stick to the perfect, home-for-the-holidays side?

Emery turned to me — he seemed more concerned about my response than I was about his. Given he had been the father to raise Bella, I knew this had to sting a little. No matter how much he did, it wasn't enough because he wasn't her biological parent.

As if reading my mind, she quickly added, "I am thankful for my Dad-Dad, and everything you've done for me. I love you, and I'm not trying to replace you."

"Oh, you're really laying it on thick, huh?" Emery said.

"I mean it," she said. "But I'm tired of acting like my other Dad is a secret to be ashamed about or something."

Heat rushed all over, and my nerves bounced all over the place. Control of this situation — of our perfect Christmas holiday break — slipped through my fingers. I pulled on my seatbelt, then turned to scowl at Bella, who was sitting cross-legged in the backseat, smushed between bags and luggage.

"What are you talking about?"

Bella shrugged. She looked up from her phone, meeting my glare. "I want to see my Dad's family. One of my cousins—Aiden— found me online, and we've been talking—"

"You've been what?" I shrieked. This was not part of the divine design, not one bit! "Wait, what? You've been talking to some strange guy on the internet? Bella."

"Aiden is my cousin."

"How do you know?"

"I believe him. Why would somebody lie about being related to me?"

"How were you able to confirm he's actually your cousin?" Emery asked.

"You know how crazy it is out there. People will scam over anything," I said. "And all this trafficking stuff happening, you never know if someone has evil intentions."

"All we talk about is our family, nothing else. He doesn't even know where I go to school."

"Who knows what he can do with the little information you have given him. We've talked about this Bella, over and over again, I tell you to watch yourself online."

Bella played with her phone, glancing out the window and shaking her head.

"I knew you wouldn't understand."

"Understand what?"

"You keep changing the subject. I've tried to ask you about my Dad so many times. So many times. But you ignore me. You act like he never existed. He didn't even do anything wrong!"

I pointed toward Emery. "He's your Dad."

"You know what I mean."

"It's complicated."

"How?"

"I-I..."

Oh my God, how much longer did we have in this car together? Forget being cornered, being stuck in a car with a know-it-all teenager, and a non-confrontational husband who loved us unconditionally made for the most awkward setting.

"They do a special memorial thing for him every Christmas since he passed away, and my cousin invited me to come this year."

"You mean to tell me *this whole time* you have been scheming behind our backs to meet with some strange boy...

from the internet?" I heard my voice climbing louder and louder with each word, and took a deep breath. Pinching the bridge of my nose, I prayed I could keep a headache from coming on, but the throbbing came anyway.

"Hey, Nell." Emery said my name in the calm and kind way he does when he wants to still me before I let the storm inside loose. I looked his way, and he mouthed, "It's okay."

I don't know if he thought giving her permission to hang out with these strangers was okay, or if he was trying to reassure me that I would be okay.

"Why are you so mad about that? It's not like I said I wanted to move to Aurbor Grove. I want to go to one event. That's it."

Speechless and without a valid argument, I stared at my daughter. The being who not only had my golden brown skin tone, high cheekbones, and wild, curly hair but also my stubbornness and apparently my skills of cornering people to get them to do what I wanted them to do.

Done with our conversation, she stuffed earbuds in her ears and looked out the window at the blur of gray highway and greenery swooshing by.

I turned back around in my seat, arms crossed. I felt Emery glancing over at me now and again. My husband was a fixer, but he couldn't do much while driving. He reached across the console, grabbed my hand, and squeezed it. He must have glimpsed the tears rolling down my cheeks.

This trip was ruined before it even began.

On paper, returning home sounded like a fine idea. I cherry-picked moments from my past to replicate — like when I went ice skating with my high school friends Ramona and Jasmine. I planned for us to grab breakfast at Rosa Mae's Cafe because that's what you did on mornings when you didn't have anywhere to be because the owner would talk your ear off if you let her.

There were many things I left off the list, though. They brought back too many bad memories and negative emotions.

I didn't include the church candlelight service they always had on Christmas morning because that would make me recall when church members attempted to kick my family and me out because I got pregnant. These days, discussions around teen pregnancy are more nuanced but back then, things were different. A group at our church threatened to kick my family and me out if I didn't stand before the congregation and confess my sins before everyone.

Pastor Brooks, my friend Jasmine's Dad, preached a sermon from John 8 on Jesus asking, "He that is without sin among you, let him first cast a stone at her." The whole congregation was tight and tense. That hushed some of the whispers, but the blows had been struck, and the wounds remained tender.

When Bella asked if we could attend the Christmas production at the theater on Broad, I made up some excuse. Going there would force me to recall how the director stripped me of my starring role after she found out I was 17 years old with a 9-month-old at home. She said she didn't want people to get the wrong idea that she was glorifying teen pregnancy.

I didn't even mention taking a ride out to Lake Coweta for the parade of Christmas trees on Christmas Eve, where various organizations showcased their lush green Leland Cypresses decked out in themed decorations. That was the last place I saw Bella's father, Tony, before he left to join the Marines.

It was next to one of those towering trees, twinkling with blue and pink lights, that he shared that he had to leave me, so that he could take better care of us. I didn't want him to go— we didn't have much of anything except each other. Actually, we had nothing but the disdain and disappointed stares of family and strangers alike.

Before having Bella, we were two teenagers "on the right

track," and we both wanted to find our way back to that place where we made folks proud of us.

So he left Aurbor Grove. And he never came back.

So I left too.

Why in the world did I think it was a good idea to come back now?

* * *

The mood shifted when Bella asked about Tony — within and around me. I rarely thought of Tony or his family.

Bella was right, he didn't do anything wrong per se, but hearing his name put me in a time machine and jetted me back to a time and place where I felt so very low. So down. So hopeless.

Tony did his best to care for us financially while my mom helped me with Bella as I attended college.

Those two years were so hard. And then came the war, and our family was on the losing end.

"Alright, here we are," Emery announced with a satisfied sigh that pulled me back to the present. "Babe, this town is really nice. Almost like those places on the movies the two of you watch all the time. You made it sound like it was all backwoods."

"It's alright," I muttered.

I imagined we'd never return to the happy-go-lucky vibe that had carried us before Bella's question.

Some of it automatically rushed back on putting our feet down on the Aurbor Grove Inn grounds. The two-story house dripped with icicle lights. Candy canes lined the walkway leading to the front door, flanked with two frosted, miniature Christmas trees draped in lights and gold ornaments.

Like a little kid, I sat in one of the rocking chairs, hugging the crimson-red pillow.

"Oh, I could stay out here all day."

"I bet you could," Emery said, lugging our bags onto the porch. He wiped his boots on the black and red welcome mat, declaring, "It's Christmas Time, Y'all!"

I put on an extra thick Southern accent. "I am a Southern lady, after all."

Bella rolled her eyes, those white buds still stuffed in her ear canals—but she heard me, though. She hadn't said a word since I refused to participate in her interrogation.

When did kids start talking so smart, anyway? These days they get all in your business and dare to ask questions I would never even *think* to ask my parents, God rest their souls.

I blamed myself for encouraging her to be strong and opinionated—that was for when she was out in the world, not for me.

"I don't know about you two, but I'm ready to get this stuff in here and get something to eat," Emery said. "I spotted the barbecue spot you said we needed to try."

"I'm starving," Bella mumbled, looking in his direction and continuing to ignore me. "Do you know if they have any vegan options?"

"Uh, vegan at a soul food barbecue spot in South Georgia?" Emery frowned at our daughter as if she'd asked for $100 million — which was just as impossible as her vegan options request.

"When did she become vegan?" He whispered to me.

I opened my mouth to say something, then shut it and shrugged my shoulders. I felt this was less about her health and more about being as ornery and aggravating as possible.

After checking in, we freshened up in our separate rooms.

"So, what do you think about all this going to meet Tony's family stuff?" I asked, applying a fresh coat of mascara.

"It's understandable."

"But just the idea of her going behind our backs to talk to this 'cousin,'" I said, throwing up air quotes.

"That's the world we live in. It's so easy to find and connect with people. Maybe if we check things out first and go with her..."

We made eye contact in the bathroom mirror, and he stopped talking. Emery knew I didn't want to do this, and once my heart and mind settled on something, there was no turning back.

"I just wanted this to be something for us. Just us. No drama. No extra mess."

"It doesn't have to be that way."

"Oh, digging in the attic that is my past in Aurbor Grove is nothing but a mess."

Emery wrapped his arms around me and pecked my shoulder.

"Our daughter is growing up. You don't have much family on your side. She knows my side all too well. She wants to know more about the man she can't even remember. Can you imagine what that's like? To not be able to pull any memories of your father?"

I hadn't considered that. Despite losing my father at a young age to a car accident, the void would feel different if I couldn't draw upon the good memories.

"I'll think about it. I have a few things to prep for our class reunion on Friday, so I don't want to be so distracted that I drop the ball on that."

"Let's get through dinner at the BBQ spot that probably does not have any vegan options," he said, and I burst out laughing.

He offered another peck, this time on my lips. "It's going to be okay."

That was the thing about Emery, when he said that, I

believed him. I knew he wasn't just saying that to get me to shut up or gloss over my angst. He would do whatever it took to ensure it.

* * *

"I'm just going to put it out there." I paused, playing with the barbecue-stained wet wipes on the picnic table. "I don't think you should meet with Jaden—"

"Aiden," Bella corrected, speaking loudly over the blues music pouring from the speaker.

"Jaden-Aiden-whoever, we don't know him. Look, it's been a while, years, since I've been here. I haven't talked to Tony's family—"

"You call him Tony?" she asked, a glint of excitement in her eyes.

"Uhm..."

"They—Aiden's family — all call him Anthony. They have a thing for names that begin with the letter A."

Now that I think about it, she was correct. I always called him Tony, but all his family members had names that began with an A. Anita, his mom, Alaya and Amanda, his sisters, and his Aunt Alma. And there was his weird cousin Aristotle — a truly eccentric guy who loved sharing his conspiracy theories with us at every family function.

I could hear Aristotle's raspy voice now: *"Let me tell you about that fake, Hollywood 'moon landing' stunt. They don't want you to know the truth. You wanna know why? I'm gonna tell you why."*

"Back to what I was saying. One day, we're going to make this happen. But this week, I want us as a family to connect and stick together. I don't want you going off by yourself with a bunch of strangers."

"My family."

I sighed deeply. This girl would not stop. "*Your* family."

"But why not?"

"It's just — we...I have so many things to do for the class reunion, and when I'm not wrapping up those details, I'll be creating Christmas memories with you and your Dad." I nodded at Emery, who I realized was watching me with a funny expression. "This is about our family."

"Okay," she muttered, pushing her plate away. The only evidence that food once sat on it were the clean rib bones and maybe a tablespoon of cold, baked macaroni and cheese.

I hoped she'd let go of this whole family reunion idea as quickly as she'd given up on veganism upon smelling the savory scent of smoked pork billowing in the air around The Que.

We only had time for one reunion — the class of 2001.

"Okay?" I confirmed.

"I said okay," she grumbled. "Don't get loud and embarrass me."

Emery looked between the two of us. So often he played referee. Poor guy. I knew the one thing that could bring us all together on the same page.

"I'm thinking about ordering some banana pudding to go. Are y'all down for some dessert?"

"Do you really have to ask?" Bella's lips curved up into a wide smile.

That's my girl.

* * *

December 20, 2016

As planned, we woke up early the next morning to grab breakfast at Rosa Mae's Cafe.

Whatever frustrations and arguments we had melted away after a couple of servings of her cinnamon rolls.

"Before we leave," Bella began, pausing to lick stickiness from her thumb and forefinger, "I have to get a dozen of these to take home with me."

After spending the day shopping in the boutiques downtown, Bella seemed like her normal self.

We laughed and criticized each other's fashion choices and gift-wrapping abilities. I was more of a carefully measure, fold and create neat lines wrapper and she was more of a tape-it-all-together type. Whatever she bought Emery had an odd, bunched-up corner.

She actually requested a second night of dinner at The Que. We got to-go plates and enjoyed smoked chicken wings, brisket, and pulled pork on the porch of the Aurbor Grove Inn.

"This used to be the spot in our house. Every evening we'd sit on the porch, watch people come and go. My grandma knew everybody's business," I said, rocking back and forth.

Watching the skyline transform from bright yellows and oranges to pink and purple, we were the family I'd envisioned us to be.

"Do you think God ever gets bored of painting a masterpiece sunset every evening?" Emery asked, gazing at the sky with reverence.

"Every day gets a new design," I said. "It may have similar colors, but there are always tweaks and little changes that make each day its own. Like a good designer, God knows the perfect place for every little detail."

"Even when it looks like a mess to us," Emery said.

"Look at ya'll being all poetic and spiritual. Is this what sitting on a porch does to you?" Bella mocked, pointing a finger.

I tossed a balled-up napkin her way.

"There is something about being home. About being on the ground where your roots are. You should cherish it." I couldn't tell if Emery was advising me or Bella, so I tucked his wisdom away.

I invited them to keep the family fun going and join me and Ramona at the Jingle Bell Festival. Emery wanted to catch up on work, and Bella said she needed a nap after such a long day and too much meat.

"Chicken has this ingredient in it — tryptophan — it makes you sleepy," she said.

"Girl, where do you get all of this stuff from?" I laughed.

Full from all the goodness, I walked two miles downtown to the Festival. Bella may have been onto something because if I hadn't been on my feet, I would have passed out on the bed too.

I met Ramona at the main gazebo, decorated with garland, white lights, and little red bows.

"Nell, was the Jingle Bell Festival this much fun when we were in school?" Ramona asked.

The two of us strolled slowly throughout downtown Aurbor Grove. Main Street and Broad were the nexus of most of the activities. Vendors, food trucks, and plenty of people laughing and enjoying the holiday season crowded the space.

It was cold for South Georgians, so Ramona showed up in a red turtleneck and a thick, khaki-colored poncho. I appreciated the briskness and was fine with my thin sweater dress and boots.

"It was fun for what we could afford back then," I said. "I only did the free activities. That's why when the school bought us tickets to go ice skating, I thought it was the best time ever."

"Even though you couldn't skate a lick," Ramona said, cackling.

"That was an important part that made it equally hilarious and painful."

"Listen, I am glad to get out tonight. I have this emergency board meeting tomorrow and then it's all hands on deck for this class reunion. This is on top of my regular work," Ramona said.

"I can only imagine. I had to plan months in advance to make sure my team could cover for me these two weeks. You deserve a real vacation."

"What's that?" Ramona asked, stroking her chin dramatically as if in deep thought. "What is this vacation you speak of?"

"Do you see how you're talking crazy? That's the first sign you need a vacation."

"Ooh, they have a hot chocolate bar. If I can't get my vacation, I will settle for a temporary reward."

The line for the hot chocolate bar was one of the longest, but looking at the descriptions of the menu items, it was obvious why. All of the items sounded luxurious and just plain delicious.

Just as we joined the winding line, a customer tried to squeeze between us but cut too close, spilling her steaming treat onto me.

"I am so, so sorry," the woman apologized.

"I'll go get napkins," Ramona said, rushing away.

I patted the fabric with my hand. Maybe it wouldn't stain too much. I expected the stranger to offer to help, but when she stood there in silence, I looked up.

"Hey, Nell," she said when I realized who she was.

"Amanda?"

Tony's baby sister was only a few years younger than us, so she had to be in her late 20s now. I could never forget her eyes —before he left, they shined bright, then when he died, they dimmed to a dark sadness that reflected all of our grief. Even now, it lingered, no matter how much she smiled.

"You came," Amanda said. Her eyes darted over my shoulder.

"She's not here." The excited expression instantly switched to disappointment. "She's here in Aurbor Grove, just not at the Festival."

A small smile crept on her lips, and she looked down. She balanced the drink in one hand and used the other to wipe at her eyes.

"Aiden?" I asked.

"He's my nephew—Alaya's son."

So Aiden was real.

"You have no idea how long I've been waiting to meet her. None. I've been praying and praying. My brother...he..."

"You don't have to." I had no idea where this conversation was going, but all of the directions I thought of were not avenues I wanted to travel. Not right now.

I didn't want to revisit the time in my life when seemingly everyone turned their backs on my daughter and me.

Amanda placed a gloved hand on top of my bare ones and squeezed. "You are still my sister. No matter what. I love you."

Three very simple words that held a depth I could feel in my bones. She meant it.

Wetness glistening at the corners of her eyes, she shook her head and chuckled.

"I'm a mess at the thought of meeting her. Can you imagine how I'll be when I actually see her?"

She assumed it was a done deal based on whatever conversations Bella had with Aiden. And all I tried to do was keep it from happening. Guilt gurgled in my belly.

"Aiden showed me her pictures online, but you know there's nothing like in person. I want to hear her voice. Can she sing like Anthony?"

I smiled. "She cannot."

"I don't care. She can still join in our caroling, sing every note off-key, and I'll be proud to call her my niece," Amanda said, clapping her hands together.

"I have to say your response makes me feel like this is actually a good idea."

Amanda dug in her bag and brought out a twenty.

"Your cup of hot chocolate is on me. I recommend the dark chocolate peppermint with caramel drizzle."

"You don't have to do that."

"Yes, I do, sis. 'Cause we need to catch up on everything." She gave me a half hug. "Besides, I do not believe in enjoying hot chocolate alone. Tell Ramona I'm buying her a cup too."

"Wait, you know Ramona?"

"Girl, who doesn't know Ramona? All of my little cousins, nieces, and nephews attend her programs at the Youth Empowerment Center."

"Y'all talking about me?" Ramona appeared with a stack of napkins and a suspicious squint.

* * *

"That went way better than I thought it would," I said. Ramona slowly pulled into the driveway of the Aurbor Grove Inn. The bright lights filtered in through the windshield, turning the interior green and red.

"It was good to talk, laugh, and drink calories like no one was watching," Ramona chuckled.

"We all know holiday calories don't count."

"Yes, this is very true."

I yawned, unbuckling my seatbelt. "I'm so glad you were with me today."

Ramona's eyebrows knitted together, as I became a blubbering fool. I'm talking tears, snot bubbles, everything.

"Hey, hey, what's wrong?" She fished for a pack of Kleenex and handed me a couple to dry my eyes, then blow my nose.

"I had this picture-perfect image of what it would be like to come back home with my picture-perfect family. I was gonna show 'em."

"Show who?"

"That's the thing. It was silly." I hunched my shoulders. "I don't know what's wrong with me."

Ramona shook her head. "No, don't say that. You felt the way you felt for a reason. It was very real. Church hurt is very real."

"You remember how it all went down. I mean, you and Jasmine were the only ones that really stood by my side. Everybody else's parents told them to beware, I was a bad influence."

"You know how it is — people can say hurtful things without thinking about the pain they're causing."

"I realized that I'd been holding on to a lot of anger. Resentment. And just plain sadness from years and years ago. And I allowed that to keep my daughter away from her family because I didn't want to deal with it. I didn't want her to see that part of my life when we were poor—so poor—and struggling. I wanted to cover it up, make us look pretty and perfect."

"She doesn't need perfect. She needs you to be you — her mom. It's not our success, our jobs, or our money that makes it special. It's the love."

"Let me find out you're a part-time motivational speaker." I jokingly slapped her shoulder. "Thanks for the word."

"I do what I can."

"Alright, let me get in here. Emery already texted me 50-11 times."

Ramona idled in her car until I made it inside. Each step of the staircase creaked as I made my way up.

Emery had stretched out on the too-short couch, and fallen asleep, mouth wide open while the TV blared ESPN.

"I'm back!"

He jolted awake. "How was it hanging with Ramona?"

"It was nice. And in a very ironic moment, I ran into Tony's sister Amanda."

"Oh, really now?" He sat up, leaning forward with interest.

"If you could have seen the excitement she had on her face at the thought of seeing my baby…"

"She probably hasn't seen her since she was a baby-baby."

"So we talked, and I felt good by the end of the night. I explained how everything went down and why I left, and she understood it. They want to be in Bella's life. She said that not having her around has been a big void for them."

"It's crazy because Bella felt that same way."

"Right! Everything fell into place — "

"Like it was supposed to," he finished my sentence. "Even if it wasn't quite what you 'planned,' there is a divine plan in play."

"I am so proud of her for pushing for what she needs. I would have given up."

"Maybe back then, but not anymore. You're where she learned it from."

"I was going to wait until tomorrow, but I'm too excited to sleep," I said. "I have to tell her now."

I skipped out of the room and down the hallway.

I tapped lightly on the cream-colored door bearing the room name in a gold script against a black placard: The Rose Room.

"Bella?" I said softly.

I know this girl hasn't fallen asleep at 11 pm. I knocked again.

What was taking so long?

"Hey, can you open up?"

That's when my Mama-intuition kicked into high gear. I didn't hear her shuffling across the room. The TV was on, but no other signs of life.

I rushed back to our room to get the extra key for her room, Emery right in front of me.

Entering that room and seeing everything left in such as mess, but Bella missing, everything became a whirlwind.

"Where is she? Where did she go? Where?"

Emery's mouth opened, and he shook his head. "She didn't tell me she was leaving or anything." He checked his phone. "She didn't send me a message."

"Where is she?" I screamed.

"Babe, babe, just give me a minute," he said.

"What if she went out trying to find Aiden on her own or something? She doesn't know this town. What if she got lost?"

"She has that app on her phone. I can pull up her location." He tapped and swiped. "There we go."

We rushed downstairs and hopped in the car. Emery handed me his phone, the app open, and pinging Bella's location.

"I'll pull up the address on GPS," he said.

It should have comforted me that we had an idea of where she might be, but what state would I find her in?

* * *

"You've arrived at your destination," the GPS announced.

"What in the..." Emery's voice trailed as he slowed down, the gravel crackling under the wheels.

I recognized this place vaguely but didn't immediately connect the dots as to why my daughter would come here. Or was she kidnapped and taken here? As the headlights flooded the dark graveyard, I glimpsed movement.

"There she is."

She wasn't alone.

I ran through those gates like the high school track star I once was and clutched her in my arms. "Bella." I felt all over her body, searching for what I don't know.

"Mom. I'm okay. Geez."

"What were you thinking? You had us scared to death!"

Emery finally jogged up, bending over to breathe. "Dang, Flo-Jo."

"Why do you have her out here in the middle of the night!" I yelled, turning my attention to a lanky, teenager, I assumed was Aiden.

"I-I-I-I-" He raised his palms in a surrender motion, his eyes bugging.

The fear on his face let me know that he was as innocent as Amanda proclaimed him to be.

"Or did she rope you into this?"

"How did you even get here?" I asked.

"We took an UBER," Bella said, a hint of pride in her voice as she waved her phone.

"You want to be grown so bad." I took another step forward, ready to remind her that I was the adult and she was the child, when she stuck out her arm and yelped, "It's bad luck to step on people's graves. That's my Dad's grave."

I froze.

"You-you came to visit his grave?"

Of course. How did I miss that? My brain stopped working the moment I thought my child was in danger.

"When you said I couldn't attend the family get-together, I had to do something. I couldn't be here and not do something, anything. I'm the one that convinced Aiden to come with me, not the other way around."

"Son, walk with me to the car so we can call your Mama."

Emery waved Aiden along. "I'll tell her we're bringing you home."

"Yes, sir."

Usually, kids feared his towering frame and booming voice more than me, but I guess I let the storm out, thundering and clapping so much that Aiden would do anything to get away from me. The way my emotions were brewing inside of me, I didn't blame him.

"Bella..." I began, struggling to find the words. "You can't just go off like this. You're sixteen."

"You were sixteen when you got pregnant with me, and you're telling me you never went off by yourself to places."

"That's exactly the reason why I don't want you to. I don't want you to make the same mistake—" I cut myself short before I let the words tumble out of my mouth. "I made choices that led to certain blesses and consequences. Anything I tell you to do, it's because, baby, I want you to be blessed."

I couldn't clean it up, and my words fell on deaf ears, the ache and longing visible on my daughter's face.

"Come here." I hugged her, clung to her, even as her arms hung limply by her side. "I love you. He loved you."

"Why don't you ever talk about him?" she cried, her words muffled onto my shoulder. "You act like he never existed."

I pulled away because I wanted her to look me in the eyes when I confessed. "I was wrong about that. I was still dealing with my own stuff. And I let that affect you. But it's okay."

"You're going to tell me about him?"

"Yep." I clasped her fingers between mine. "I'm going to tell you all about him. And your Auntie Amanda and your Grandma Anita, they're going to tell you some things too."

"Mom!" She gasped so loudly I swore the crickets hushed. Squeezing tightly to my hand, she jumped up and down.

"Can we get out of this creepy graveyard? Your cousin Aristotle said they have aliens buried out here."

"Wait, what?"

"Oh, I'm sure you'll find out all about him tomorrow too."

* * *

December 21, 2016

"Bella, are you sure you still want to do this?"

"I do. I think so."

"Sweetie, we are here for you no matter what," Emery said, looking over his shoulder.

Bella rubbed her hands up and down her thighs, glancing furtively at the door.

"Do you want me to come in with you? Stay a little while?" She silently nodded, biting her bottom lip.

Amanda and her family must have been watching us because the door flung open as soon as we made it to the top step. She was flanked by a much older woman and one who could have passed as her twin.

They looked at both of us, but she spoke directly at Bella. "We are so glad you're here."

An awkward silence hung in the air, then finally, the elder woman waved us inside. "Y'all come on in out the cold."

"Yes, ma'am," Bella said. The fluffy, black poof on her head seemed to weigh her down. She kept her hands clasped in front of her. I rubbed her back reassuringly.

"I'm going to stay with her for a little while," I said. "If that's okay." I don't know why I added that knowing good and well, I didn't care if they approved of my presence or not, I was staying with my child.

"I'm Anita, your-your grandmother."

"I'm your Aunt Amanda."

"And I'm your Aunt Alaya."

In a move that surely shocked all of us, Bella reached out and hugged them all in one swoop of an arm.

"I'm Arabella." I hadn't referred to her as such since...since she was three. She wanted to own her "A" too, I guess.

"Oh," Mrs. Anita gasped. She closed her eyes, and when she reopened them, tears brimmed the bottom. Alaya sniffled, and Amanda observed my daughter in awe.

"I'm sorry I keep staring, but you look just like him."

It was true. Somehow, Bella came out looking like me but grew into Tony's features — his pointy nose, almond-shaped eyes, long lashes, and thick, bow-like lips.

"It's crazy, isn't it?" I said. I took a step forward, following them into the living room, but Bella hung back. She grabbed my elbow.

"Mom, I think I'm okay."

I held onto both of her shoulders. "Are you sure? I can stay. I don't mind."

I never had any complaints about Tony's family — we always counted them as good people, but still, I was leaving my heart in the hands of strangers.

"I'm sure. I—" She looked toward them, then back at me. "I can't explain it. I know I don't know them very well, but they feel like family."

"That's because they are, baby." I kissed her cheek and held her close. "You call me if anything, I mean, any*thing* feels off."

"I will."

"Okay, baby, I love you." With one final hug, I slowly left the foyer. When I shut the door, the wreath's jingle bells jangled.

"Is she alright?" Emery asked, eyeing me as I eyed the door. The car hummed as the heat filled the cabin.

"She's good."

"Are you alright?"

"I'll be just fine."

"Are we heading back to the Inn, or are we staking it out."

I gave him a look.

"Stakeout it is. I brought snacks."

He reached into the back seat, pulling out chips, nuts, candy canes, and apples.

I grabbed a candy cane, biting the hook first. "I think he would be proud of her."

"He'd be proud of you, too," Emery said.

My breath hitched as I tried to hold back the tears. Nobody ever told me that, and I needed to hear it.

For so much of my life, I tried to prove that I was worthy, wasn't some statistic, and did a good job.

My daughter—*Ara*bella Michelle Devereaux-Rogers—was my living legacy. She was evidence of the love that had carried us from those dark moments to the here and now. Hope was never lost. It was embedded in her DNA, and everything she touched bore the mark of a mother and two fathers who always did their best to take care of her.

I reached over and grabbed Emery's hand. "We did a good job, babe."

The Big Christmas Payback

Ramona

These kids are gonna have me drinking before noon. I kid. I kid.

Before anybody even thinks about calling the Department of Family and Children Services on me, this is me being my dramatic self.

I don't even drink. I like to eat my calories.

Well, unless I'm drinking hot double chocolate peppermint with caramel drizzle, that's a caloric bomb worth having.

This isn't even one of my worst days, but we're only getting started. Talk to me in five hours, and I may want to re-rank December 21, 2016, up there with May 10, 2005, my first day working full-time here at the Youth Empowerment Center, YEC for short.

Even though I'd volunteered for years, knew the staff well, and cherished the kids, when I was hired as an official employee, a switch flipped somewhere in everybody's minds, apparently.

I don't know what it was, but it felt like the first day the character Miss Celie arrived at Mr.'s house in the Color Purple movie — including the Harpo throwing the rock and creating a gash scene. But in my case, a kid threw a stapler.

Today reminded me of that kid. No, there weren't any staplers flying, but the vibe was chaos times a thousand.

I touched my temple, where a tiny half-dollar scar served as a souvenir of that special day and my commitment to this center and my kids.

On a regular day, if a stranger stopped by YEC, the scenes and sounds would probably overwhelm them. It was organized chaos.

The smell of fruit cups mingled with glue, sweat, and general teen funk; balls bouncing in the gym while our basketball squad practiced; our drama team flouncing around in costumes cobbled together from donations and construction paper; our study hall filled with kids of all ages, clinging to the one-on-one attention our volunteers showered them with that they couldn't get in huge classes; our teen leaders playing and fussing over video games — they created; our young ones simply running or playing some contest they made up having pure, unadulterated fun with no adult telling them to shut up, sit down, or somehow fit into their box of how children should be.

They were *my* kids.

There were so many negative headlines, gossip, and good old-fashioned contempt for the younger generation. Even some people at my church — good, "anything is possible with God" types—claimed they were too far gone.

I refused to give up on *my* kids. I refused to abandon the village.

As for this foolishness today, where the noise and rowdiness were times a thousand, I blamed the candy. They were all getting an extra dose of sugar with the end-of-the-semester holiday celebrations and family get-togethers. Shoot, most of them are probably still eating on their Halloween stash.

We, too, contributed to this problem. The smell of vanilla and buttery dough floated throughout the Center as volunteers and students made and decorated Christmas Cookies to sell as a fundraiser during the Jingle Bell Festival.

That's the thing about October through December, you can expect things to get extra because of all the sweets and treats that come with the season.

They're so high on high fructose, how can they pay attention? And for whatever reason, they're more open to trying all of the ideas they'd spent 30 seconds considering.

Like going on a sleigh ride with boxes down a hill minus snow. It wasn't even that cold outside.

"What's going on with you, Cece?"

"Mrs. Ramona, I didn't even do anything," she mumbled, sucking her teeth.

"I saw you on the 'sleigh.' You and Michael. He's at the doctor right now with a sprained wrist. And you could have been hurt too. What I want to know is how did you get into the office to get the supplies?"

The office chair squeaked as I leaned onto my desk—okay, onto the stacks and stacks of file folders atop my desk. My gesture to get closer to the crossed-armed teenager only made the girl scoot back. She played with one of the jet-black braids that fell to her waist, picking at the wispy end, then moved on to another. Cece's eyes studied the strands intently, as if I didn't exist.

"The door requires a key card. Ms. Janice is missing her badge."

"Michael took it."

"Are you saying that because he can't defend himself?"

"No, I'm telling the truth. *Bruh.*"

I narrowed my eyes and pursed my lips, willing myself to see this thing through with a straight and serious face.

"So you're telling me if we search his pockets right now, we'll find Ms. Janice's badge?"

"Yeah. No. I mean, I dunno."

"I can see the badge bulging out of your pocket right now." I pointed a finger at her khaki pants.

Guilt flashed on her face for maybe five seconds, then she suddenly switched gears.

"Ohhh, that's what you're looking for. I think it came out of Michael's pocket when we were playing around. Yep. That's probably what happened." She was making it all up as she went, and I blinked dramatically at her commitment to this role of 'innocent bystander.'

"And-and so, then I picked it up. I was bringing it in here to give to you because I couldn't find Ms. Janice. I didn't know he had stole it. I promise."

"Little girl," I mumbled. "C'mon now."

"I'm serious." She widened her eyes and stretched her arms to showcase sincerity. I knew Cece was a great singer but made a note that she might be great for the drama program too.

"We don't lie. We don't steal. We don't—"

"...hurt each other," Cece finished the words, I repeated to students over and over again.

"That's the deal, right?"

"Yes, ma'am."

"When you lie, steal, and hurt other people, you hurt yourself most," I reminded her. "I'll take this badge back to Ms. Janice, but I want you to apologize to her before you go to choir practice."

"Okay, I will," she said. "Mrs. Ramona, you look cute today. Where are you going?"

"Don't try to change the subject!" I said, pointing a finger. I adjusted the golden yellow blazer I'd worn for my board meeting. Usually, I was casual in a YEC polo shirt and slacks. "I do look cute, though."

My phone dinged, alerting me that I had fifteen minutes before our board meeting. "Go find Ms. Janice — but I'm going to talk to your mom and dad about what happened today. This isn't over."

Cece hopped up and headed out, then turned on her heel.

"You might wanna take that off before you go to your meeting." She tapped the top of her head and motioned for me to touch my own.

"Oh, yeah." I snatched the red and white Santa hat I'd worn for story time off my head and tossed it on top of my manila folders.

Truthfully, I preferred the hyped-up kids over the board meetings, where people droned on and on about everything. I understood where the kids were coming from. I saw their potential and the possibilities.

When it came to the board stuff, I felt claustrophobic, like they were trying to box me in. They cared about the kids but mostly from a numbers perspective — attendance, graduation rates, any and every statistic you could think of.

Now, I believed those things had tremendous value, but I was more concerned with *why* the numbers were what they were than doing all that maneuvering to make things "look" better vs. being better.

I had a feeling that's what the "emergency board meeting" would be about: a bunch of numbers. I loved our volunteers and our leaders, but some of them didn't care much about the other details.

Like how I knew Chase Dornan's grandmother's passing had deeply affected him, and as we awaited approval and funds to pay for counseling, I had bought a few sessions for him out of my own pocket.

YEC was for the youth, yes, but I also made sure parents had access to the computer lab so they could apply for jobs and take nutrition, emotional intelligence, and financial literacy classes. What was the point of empowering kids with the knowledge and tools to live full and healthy lives, then sending them home to adults who hadn't acquired the skills yet?

They only saw that the school identified Tanisha Lawrence as behind in her reading and literacy, but I knew she devoured books that included characters she could relate to, so I bought her one of her favorites to read for every classic title she finished and scored an A on her Accelerated Reading quiz.

Our board members, especially Debra Cunningham, expressed outrage at the outbreaks of fights at the school and the surrounding neighborhoods, wondering if YEC was contributing to the problem somehow by gathering so many different groups of people in one place. But I knew YEC was the one safe space everyone could come and know violence wasn't tolerated.

I brought up these things whenever I could, but it was always a fight, and sometimes I felt like I was the only one advocating for the kids. That only brought on more responsibilities, meetings, and visits with parents to explain our program guidelines. *No good deed goes unpunished, right?*

I was so busy doing the work, I had very little time to keep up with all the administrative stuff, which was fairly new to me.

I was in my role as Executive Director for almost a year now, and I still hadn't gotten a full handle on the politics and proper prioritizing.

For example, instead of preparing for my board meeting by pulling the latest reports, I was sending emails to students' parents, like Cece's mom and dad, and now I was late.

I gathered my padfolio, YEC tumbler half-way full of coffee, and rushed out the office door, jogging through the hallway. I ran into a few of my babies, and they stopped to hug me.

I slowed down to a stroll when I approached the room where our YEC choir was practicing for the Jingle Bell Festival's Youth Night Extravaganza. Each year, community youth groups were recognized, celebrated, and given donations to support their programs. Having a good performance during the concert would attract more attention—and funding.

We had a small, but talented group of singers and musicians. Their sweet, harmonic rendition of "O Holy Night" lulled me to a place of peace in the chaos.

I stopped in my tracks, listening for a few seconds as Joey's adolescent-on-the-verge-of-becoming-a-teen voice belted out my favorite part: *Fall on your knees. Oh hear the angel voices...*

Our volunteer leader Matt, cut him short. "Let's do that again, with more *oomph*. This is the part in the song to really get people's hearts."

Ding! This time my phone was reminding me I was ten minutes late to the board meeting. As I went to take a sip of coffee to give me the boost I was going to need, I felt a splash against my hand.

"What in the world?" I muttered. The cold drop ran down my wrist. Just as I looked up, I spied another drop heading my way. It caught me right in my left eye.

The roof was leaking...again. I'd have to go to the other side of the building to find a bucket in the storage room. I thought about asking Matt to take care of it, but I didn't want to interrupt their practice.

"Mrs. Ramona."

I waved. "Hey Kendrick. How are you doing today?"

"I'm good. Are you good?"

I forced a smile, ignoring all of the things that were going wrong-wrong in the moment. "I'm good."

"Are you sure?"

Concerned that maybe I needed to do a better job of hiding my frustration, I said, "I'm sure. Why would you ask?"

He held up his hand to my face. "It's like...it's like...it's like something black is running out of your eyes."

"Oh no, my mascara!" I stomped my feet, which made Kendrick jump back. "Trust me, I'm fine. I will talk to you later, young man."

I ran off to find a bucket and a bathroom to fix my makeup.

* * *

Of course, everyone was there on time, except me. Even my Assistant director, Melissa, was in her seat, fresh notebook and pen ready to take notes or orders.

"My apologies for being late. We had a little situation—well we had a few situations. I hope you understand."

Most of the people around the U-shaped table offered tight, but understanding smiles. Debra, the board member whose deep connections and pockets ensured her a certain level of power, even though she wasn't Chair, scowled. Sometimes I wondered why she even bothered to serve on the board if all she wanted to do was criticize everything.

"That's becoming more and more frequent, wouldn't you say?" she asked. "We called this meeting today because of yet another *situation*."

Our board chair, local attorney Jackson Oliver called the meeting to order, interrupting her snark with a professional and solemn tone.

"We needed to meet today because, unfortunately, we may have to shut down YEC next semester."

"Wait, what? Why? What's going on?" Befuddled, I immediately regretted taking a sip of coffee because it came tumbling back out, landing on my fancy, professional blazer.

Jackson pulled up images on the projector screen. "We knew that the center needed considerable repairs, which is why we were planning for a huge capital campaign next year, but it was brought to our attention that there are some really unsafe conditions in a few areas of the facility.

"Some kids posted pictures of what appears to be mold, the leaky roof, and the doors that won't lock online, and it's been a total frenzy. The local media picked it up, and now they're asking us questions about how we will fix it. But we don't have the funds to do so any time soon. We usually see an uptick in donations during this season, but the nonprofit space is competitive. We didn't market ourselves or do a "Giving Tuesday" campaign this year. Our numbers are down.

"But it's not all about money. The liability that comes with having kids come here with these issues is just too great." The grief on his face mirrored how I felt on the inside.

"And where have you been all day that you didn't see this trending online?" Debra chimed in.

"I-uh..."

"We've been with the kids," Melissa said. She whipped her head around, her long blond ponytail falling on her shoulder. "That's our focus as soon as we walk through the doors. We don't have time to scroll on social media or sit around and watch the morning news."

I was grateful to have her at the table to defend our work because I was still processing the images. I was aware of the roof, but *mold*? And which door was being left unlocked? It took everything in me to sit still and not go investigate these problems.

"There's no need for us to get into with each other," said Carmen, our parental representative on the board. "You all do great work with the kids, and this facility is in dire need of repair — both things can be true, and no one has to point fingers. We are all responsible."

"But only one of us is the Executive Director, correct?" Debra continued. Board members murmured at her insistence on keeping the blame bullseye on me. "I just think you're way over your head."

Oh, she wasn't going to let this go. She never wanted me for the ED job. From the get-go, she tried to convince the board to hire her niece, who worked at a larger, national youth non-profit organization. She felt we needed to move from our local model and take YEC national. While the other board members considered that strategy, they didn't go for her nepotism, wanting to hire from within.

She pounced on this opportunity to highlight my deficiencies. I guess this was payback.

"I just want to say, just like I've always done, I am willing to do whatever it takes to keep the doors of YEC wide open for every child in this community that needs it," I said. "I don't want to only focus on the problem. I need us to find a solution. Is there a way to prioritize some repairs to keep this place safe?"

"We can take a look at that," Jackson said. "It still doesn't solve for the budget. We could perhaps tap into our credit line, but that won't be enough either."

"Well, we have the Jingle Bell Festival fundraiser, where—" I began, smiling proudly at the kids and volunteers baking away as we spoke.

"That's chump change in comparison to what we need. We need $100,000, not $100," Debra interrupted with a mocking laugh.

"We should all look at ways to dig deeper in our pockets and budgets. Maybe we can double the price of the cookies and do extra promotions online," Jackson said.

"It's end of the year," Carmen began. "If any of your companies need to spend, let's encourage them to invest dollars in YEC.

The board members jumped on that bandwagon, and began to discuss their favorite topic: numbers.

Defeated, I slumped in the chair, looking back and forth between them all. Melissa furiously took notes. I waited patiently for any ideas to come to me on how *I* could save YEC. I drew a complete blank. As I tapped my pen on my notepad, a plop splashed on the paper, the blue line blurring.

Did anybody else see that? I wanted to get another bowl or bucket but didn't want to draw any additional attention to the fact that this place was falling apart, and somehow I never noticed it. I just kept working, plugging holes, and trying to Band-aid it together.

Debra was right. I was in way over my head.

* * *

I ran the numbers for the 100th time and came up with the same sum. And there was no way we would make up the difference at the Jingle Bell Festival unless we somehow sold our few hundred cookies for $250 each. Them things weren't that good.

My stomach rumbled in protest. I hadn't eaten anything all day, and now it was well after 7 pm. My husband Mark had the night off and offered to pick me up and go get dinner at the Jingle Bell Festival— there was a lobster roll food truck that I obsessed over. I didn't tell him I'd gotten a roll when I hung out with Nell.

We'd been trying to have a date night for 387 days, but there was always something happening at YEC. Tonight was no different.

I couldn't leave until I mustered the strength to write a parent letter announcing the closure of YEC for the foreseeable future.

My email inbox was filled with questions from parents, volunteers, media, and strangers asking about the social media posts featuring the worst sides of the center.

We were on the five and six o'clock local news broadcasts and likely would appear at eleven too.

Some people even found my cell phone number and left several nasty voice messages, calling me everything but a child of God. I popped online for a hot second to see the images for myself. There were so many comments, and I'd estimate half were in defense of YEC and our work. Several alumni chimed in and shared their stories. But the other half of the commentary went beyond constructive criticism into demeaning our children. And I couldn't take it. I logged off.

I pulled up my document, the cursor blinking on the white, blank screen.

Dear Parents,

As many of you are aware...

That's as far as I'd gotten since the board voted to close the center by the end of the week. Next semester, we'd focus on the capital campaign, raising funds, and completing priority repairs. We would be lucky if we could reopen by summer.

A part of me wanted to fight it and still search for some miraculous solution that could keep the student safe and in place.

As the day winded down with parent pickups, quietness fell over the center. A few students whose parents worked late nights hung around, their chatter and laughter echoing throughout the building.

Cece was one of them.

"Mrs. Ramona, they delivered this pizza and told me to bring it to you." She plopped in my chair, her mood much lighter than it had been this morning.

I perked up at seeing the box from Pisano's Pizza Place. That was Mark's favorite pizza spot. Even if we couldn't get date night together, he ensured I was good. My stomach sounded its excitement.

The long and loud growl made Cece giggle. "This came just in time for you."

"Join me for a slice." I pulled out paper plates from my drawer and cleared a space on my desk for her to pull up and eat with me.

We both munched on pepperoni and sausage pizza that was too hot, but we were too hungry and risked the scalding.

"What are you doing, Mrs. Ramona?" Cece asked, her mouth half-filled.

"A little work."

"Working on what?"

I clasped my fingers together and propped up my chin, chewing on my pizza and thoughts. "Just stuff."

"Are you still gonna tell her about what happened?"

"I sure am."

"Dag, Mrs. Ramona," she said. "My brother said you didn't play. I guess he was tellin' the truth."

"How is Isaiah doing?" That brought a smile to my face. Thinking and talking about anything else but how I and YEC was a complete failure was a welcomed conversation.

"He's doing good. He had finals yesterday, and he's coming home tonight."

"Well, make sure you tell him to stop by and say hello when he—" My voice trailed as I realized YEC wouldn't be open for him to pay a visit. All of the concerns returned: *What would happen to the kids who can't get a good meal at home? What about the ones, like Cece, whose parents worked shift hours that made it hard to find babysitters? Where would the basketball team have its games?*

Just as she finished the crispy crust, Cece's mother Carol walked briskly in my office.

"Hey, Ramona! Cece let's go."

Cece slowly got up, waiting for me to say something.

"Girl, what are you standing around for? I left my car running," Carol fussed.

For whatever reason, I didn't even feel like addressing what happened today. Maybe tomorrow. Tonight, tonight, I wanted to end things on a good note.

"Ya'll have a good night," I said, to which Cece beamed like never before. She came around the desk and gave me a big hug.

"Good night, Mrs. Ramona."

I'd given what I thought was my best and came up short. I could admit that now. Maybe Debra's niece's experience could come in handy for YEC.

I erased "Dear Parents." As I entered the date December 21, 2016, I decided this would definitely go down as my worst day at YEC.

I typed out an address to Board Chair Jackson Oliver and members, took a deep breath, and prayed for the courage to do what needed to be done.

I would like to formally submit my letter of resignation...

* * *

The next morning, the Board Chair, Jackson met me in the YEC parking lot. The sun barely peeked over the tree line so who knows how early he had arrived to catch me.

"You cannot resign."

"Good morning Mr. Oliver, how are you doing?"

"I'm sorry. Good morning." He followed behind me as I opened the front door, and walked through the long hallway to my office.

"I see the passion. And you've put in the hard work. You can't just give up now."

"What time is it now?"

"7:20."

"Do you want to know what time I got home last night?"

"Um, what?" His eyes moved back and forth, as if he was confused by where this was going.

"I got home at 11:42 pm. That's not the first time, either." I rounded the corner of my desk and sat down slowly. "My husband was in bed because that's where he usually is when I get home from working here. Either he's at work or in bed. But he and I had a long talk, and we agreed it's best I take a step back."

"Resigning isn't a step back, it's a whole step away. It's a little drastic isn't it?" Jackson asked, holding the letter in his hand. "When you emailed this to me, I knew I was supposed to share it with the other board members, but I wanted to come here and see if I could convince you to change your mind."

"It would take a Christmas miracle. Jackson, I'm...tired." My voice cracked as I said the two words that illustrated the defeat I'd felt for a long time. I wiped the rebel tear trying to escape my right eye with a finger.

"Look, I don't doubt the sacrifices you've made. I've seen them myself. You're the reason I even joined the board. I knew that investing my time, talent, and treasure here would be worth it."

"That's why I feel okay with my decision. Having people like you on the board, people who genuinely care about the kids, I'm sure you'll select an ED that can get the job done that I couldn't."

"That's the only criticism I have for you. You didn't try."

I raised an eyebrow at that. The disrespect!

"Oh, I tried. I tried and tried." Emotions rose inside of me, and I took a deep breath to calm myself.

"You tried to be the ED, Program Director, Marketing Specialist, Janitor, Chef. You cannot do it all on your own. No one can. I know you know this place better than anybody, but we, the board, need you focused on *your* job."

"Umph." That's all I could give him. "We can't afford to hire all of those people. Besides, isn't leadership doing whatever it takes to get the job done?"

"Not if it's not your job. Look, I know in nonprofits, you have to wear many hats. What I wanted you to do was to come to us and tell us you needed the help. Tell your staff and volunteers how they can pitch in. People want to be a part of the change. You can't just hog it all yourself."

"Okay, now Jackson, I know you come from a family of preachers, but you don't have to keep up this sermon."

"My bad. I'm on your side. I want to see you win. You chose to take the self-righteous route, so I had to ride with you."

"And you're just still going," I said, amazed at how he offered constructive criticism without being mean.

"And I really want to tear up this resignation letter. Will you let me see what I can do to help? Think about it for another few days, and let's figure this thing out together. It's not all on you, if you don't want it to be."

I eyed him, not verbally agreeing, but he probably saw me softening to the idea.

"And take a vacation. A real vacation. You get 20 days — how many have you taken?"

I bit my bottom lip and frowned.

"I can't take a vacation with all this stuff going on!"

"There will always be, as Debra put it, *situations*. Trust that your people, that we love YEC as much as you do."

* * *

I didn't get any sleep last night, my body tossed and turned as many times as my decision to leave YEC. Mark and I made a pros and cons list and prayed, but when the sun started pouring through my window, I still didn't have the clarity I needed.

Apparently, I did get a bit of that vacation time in as the clock read 8 am, and I was still in bed, not at my desk.

My phone rang, and the number for YEC displaying on my screen. I expected it to be Melissa, worried about my whereabouts. Instead, a different voice greeted me.

"You've got to get here now. I don't know. I don't know what to do," Cece said repeatedly. The girl sounded like she was breaking down.

"Okay, breathe, baby, breathe. I'm on my way, but tell me what's going on."

"It's the roof. It's-it's so much worse than it was. Mrs. Ramona, you've got to get here fast."

"What's wrong?" Mark asked.

"It's the Youth Center." For the first time in a long time, he didn't let out an audible sigh or roll his eyes at the place interrupting our plans together. He grabbed his keys and opened the door for me to go out before him.

"This doggone roof is going to be the end of me. Maybe it's a sign," I said, jumping in the passenger seat. "This executive director role is just too much for me. Maybe instead of leaving, I can request a demotion back to Senior Program Director. For me, it never was about a title. It's always been about the kids."

"And that's why you are in the ED position." He glanced at me while slowing down for a red light. "You know what the right priorities are: the kids."

"You can do the right things sometimes, and it doesn't matter. It's not enough. But you know what, I've learned a lot. And one day I will be ready to lead."

I never knew I could arrive to YEC so quickly. I didn't wait for Mark to open the door for me, stumbling up the steps and through the doors.

"Cece, where are you? Why are all the lights out?" Fumbling around in the dark, I reached for the switch. As soon as the bright lights flooded the gym, the crowd shouted "Surprise."

Now, I'm a Taurus all day, so this gathering, replete with balloons, cheers, and smiling faces, threw me off.

"Wha-what's going on? The roof?"

Cece broke through the center of the crowd of students, parents, and familiar faces from the neighborhood.

"It's still janky, but it hasn't caved in yet. That's the only reason we could think of to get you down here quick, fast, and in a hurry."

That's when I realized Mark hadn't rushed in alongside me. He stood behind me, arms crossed, with a satisfied smile spreading across his face.

"You were in on this?"

"You know it. They called me early this morning and told me the plan. I just needed to figure out how to keep you from coming in early."

"Wait, what *is* this?"

"It's Mrs. Ramona Appreciation Day," a voice shouted. I craned my neck to find the face to match the familiar, gruff voice.

"Isaiah? What are you doing here?"

Cece's brother, Isaiah, graduated from high school five years ago and entered pharmacy school at the University of South Carolina.

"A bunch of us heard about the roof, the supplies, everything. You always showed up for us, so we wanted to show up for you for a change," he said.

Speechless. Like I had no words. None. Everything scrambled in my mind, my heart raced, and before I could catch myself a wail leaped out of my mouth. I pressed my hand against my lips, expecting the tears to come streaming down.

Isaiah held me tight — he was much bigger, with broad, sturdy shoulders, the complete opposite of the rail-thin teenager I met many years ago. And as we held on to each other, our roles had switched. This time, I needed him. I needed that confirmation that I meant something. That the work I did was not in vain.

When I pulled away, despite the tears blurring my vision, it became clear. Isaiah wasn't the only YEC alum in the crowd. Tiffany, Jamal, Keion, Marissa...all my babies had come home.

"We wanted to start something different. So every year, during the holiday season, we're hosting a YEC reunion where any student, any staff person associated with YEC can come volunteer, spend time together, and give back to the place that changed our lives," Isaiah said.

My arms outstretched, there wasn't enough space for my current and former students, but somehow we all formed a group hug.

"I love each and every one of you. All of y'all mean the world to me."

"You mean the world to us, Mrs. Ramona!" somebody shouted, and the crowd whooped and hollered, the acoustics of the gym making it sound as loud as the fans at our basketball games.

"I told you so," Mark whispered, kissing me on the cheek. He pulled me close in his arms, and I laid my head on his chest.

"I can't believe they did this."

"Sorry to interrupt." Debra offered a tight smile and scrunched her nose. I was not going to let her stop my joy ride, but her presence was definitely a speed bump.

"I'll be back, okay?" Mark made eye contact, winking. I

knew that he would be only a few steps away if I felt my mouth going in the wrong direction.

"I never had any doubts about your leadership, Ramona. Much like you, I and the board always want to make sure we're doing our best for the kids. We want this to be a safe place for them."

"I do too."

"I only want to explain the...passion we have. It may come across as micromanaging or doubt, but I assure you that's not the case. The way you were able to bring this community together and raise more than double what we needed for the roof. Amazing. Shocking, actually."

I swallowed hard and nodded, pretending I knew exactly what she was talking about.

We had the money, no, double *the money we needed to fix the roof? How? When? Who?* The questions bounced around in my head until Debra excused herself, and I pulled Mark to the side.

"How in the world did we raise $200,000?"

Mark swept his hand in the air in the direction of the students and parents.

"The alum up a Go Fund Me fundraising page online, and everybody shared stories about how you and YEC helped them. People were happy to donate to the cause. I mean, people from all across the world gave."

"Wow, wow, wow. Y'all did all of this under my nose."

"Right up under it. It pays that you're not on social media," Mark said.

Before I could cheer and jump in his arms, Jackson approached us with an "I told you so" smile. He also had my letter in hand. I snatched it from him and tore that thing up.

"We already have a construction company who is volunteering some hours to come assess the most immediate repairs this evening," Jackson said. "And Melissa has agreed to staff the office through New Year's so you can take that vacation."

I opened my mouth to protest, but Mark spoke before I could.

"That's what I'm talking about. Finally."

Jackson waved goodbye. "Y'all have a Merry Christmas."

"You too," I said.

The "reunion" livened up quickly when someone turned on Christmas music. I watched with glee as my babies — the big ones and small ones — danced around the Christmas tree. Overcome with pride at how they'd all come together, I tried to fight the happy tears and lost.

"Well, you got your Christmas miracle," Mark whispered.

"I got that and so much more. So much more."

A Christmas Match Made In Heaven

Jasmine

"You've been waiting on me, huh?" he asked.

Brandon walked slowly toward me. Fall leaves that needed to be raked and bagged crunched under his boots.

"All day."

"I'm here before nine, as promised."

I quickly checked my Apple Watch: 8:57 am.

"Barely."

He groaned, then mimicked the disappointed pout on my face. "Don't give me that. You know I try to look out for you, and put you first always."

Without my intention or consent, my lips immediately spread into a smile.

He flashed an even brighter smile, the dimple in his left cheek winking at me.

The mix of beiges, neutrals, and browns on anybody else was plain and boring, but the colors seemed to pop on Brandon. Despite the temperatures dipping into the low 50s, his unbuttoned shirt opened up into a V that revealed enough for my imagination to go on its own trip to fantasy land.

"Can you sign right here?"

Him shoving his tablet in my face reminded me that this little exchange was all business.

He dropped the stack of boxes—customized class of 2001 party favors for our class reunion—in a thud on the step next to my bright red sneakers. My car was packed, and this was the only thing I was waiting on before hitting the road.

But was it all business? Brandon always flirted with me — at least, it felt that way.

I mean, the holiday season was hectic, but he always took his time when he delivered my packages. Between Christmas gifts and the class reunion, my online shopping habits had him dropping by almost every day. He was my most consistent "date" ever.

"Ms. Jasmine, if I don't see you before Christmas, I hope it's a good one."

"You too." He jogged back to his vehicle, but before he could lunge inside, I yelled out. "Wait, Brandon. I almost forgot. This is for you. Merry Christmas."

I handed him a Christmas card and gift card I gave to all delivery people. Although, I'd put an extra five on Brandon's gift because he was always extra kind, funny, and gentlemanly. He was perfect.

You know, one time I needed to ship back this exercise contraption I ordered one late night watching QVC, and as I complained about breaking it down, he volunteered to help?

I looked up dreamily at him. Our eyes meeting — his dark browns beaming, calling me to come closer.

"Aw, man, this is so sweet." He held the red envelope to his chest. "I was just telling my wife how I have *the best* customers. You make the late nights and early mornings worth it. Alright now. Have a good one."

"That's a way to find out if he's single," the voice mumbled in my left ear.

Caught up in the whirlwind of Brandon, I'd forgotten I was on the phone with my Mama.

"Mama." I palmed my forehead.

She'd heard all of my wonderings about Brandon's relationship status since he started delivering packages to me.

It was her who put the idea in my head that he could be a possible love interest. Granted, she'd made a joke at my expense.

"I swear the only way you're going to find a date is if God himself had him delivering your Amazon packages. You never leave the house. So if you get anybody, he either's gonna work for UPS, Fedex, Ubereats, DoorDash, or one of them."

It was true. I wanted to date, but I didn't have time to do the online stuff. And I didn't want to go back into the real-life dating pool — it had pee in it. Trust me.

"I feel like you watch too many of them Lifetime and Hallmark movies. And you definitely have your nose stuck in too many of them Chris Culpepper romance books," Mama said. She had very little encouragement for my dating life, mostly criticisms. As someone who had been married for 50 years, she couldn't fathom my inability to find at least one who was good enough.

The lazy, in-love-with-love side of me wanted my guy to pop up at my doorstep or bump into me as I inspected the ripeness of avocados at the grocery store (I never got that quite right).

"I just want *my* happy ending," I muttered, shocked that I'd let the vulnerable admission slip out. Mama must have been, too because she fell so quiet, all I could hear was her TV broadcasting her favorite show, *In the Heat of the Night,* in the background. Virgil Tibbs was fussing at Chief Gillepsie about something.

"You're going to get it. One day," Mama said. "I've been praying for heaven to send you your perfect match."

"Is God mad at your or something?" I asked.

Mama laughed. "Girl, hush."

"I halfway don't want to even show up for this reunion. Once again, with nobody on my arm. Ramona and Nell will have their husbands. I'll have me, myself, and I," I pouted, leaning against my car.

"At this point, I feel like you've probably already met your husband. Maybe the timing wasn't right or something. When's the last time you talked to Fred?"

"Mama, I gotta get on the road." I ignored the mention of my ex, who not only tried to turn a weekend stay in my basement into three months, but he also took full advantage of my bank account without my knowledge. I'd never heard of "hobosexuals" — guys who date women for a place to stay— but I found out about them with Fred.

Mama didn't know all of those details because that would have invited stern judgment of us "shacking up," which was not the case. I barely saw Fred when he lived with me. I'm convinced he invited girls over to "his place." He was basically a renter who never paid rent.

"I know he ran into some financial challenges, but maybe he's gotten his life together. Baby, you have to give people a second chance sometimes."

"What's the saying, fool me once, shame on you, fool me twice, shame on me."

"I hear you, but people change. You've changed. Don't sit up here and act like you were some perfect catch yourself!" No one, not anyone, can keep you humble like your Mama.

To convince her how unworthy Fred was, I'd have to implicate myself, so I decided to end this call instead. "Mama. I've got to go!"

"Okay, okay. Are you coming to church? Make sure you pack some church clothes."

That direction left the line silent again. It didn't matter

how old I was, that I was over 30, my mother insisted on treating me like a child.

"Hello?"

"I'm still here, Mama."

"I'm just saying Christmas is on Sunday, and we go to church on Sundays."

"Mama, I'm hanging up. I have to go."

"You right about that. I don't know why you're messing around like it's not rush hour. I know you ain't that far, but it ain't a hop, skip, and a jump neither. I can't wait to see you."

"Just as a reminder, I'm staying at the Aurbor Grove Inn. It's just easier to take care of everything with the reunion."

"Alright, baby, bye-bye. See you soon."

"I'll see you...in a couple of days." I said basically to myself because my Mama had hung up on me. I only reiterated the timing of my arrival at her house because I knew she'd try to make me feel guilty about not stopping there first.

I didn't have time. I barely would make it to check in on time to prep for the reunion party.

* * *

"I cannot believe this."

This was all a mistake. I should have known better.

Anger mingled with anxiety combusted inside me. I knew my cheeks were changing in color. Like a drop of dye in water, dark redness quickly spread. The color came only when I was exceedingly upset or happy— there was no in-between.

Red-cheeked Jasmine mostly signaled the unleashing of what friends nicknamed Jas*mean*.

"I'm so, so sorry about this misunderstanding. We upgraded our online reservation system. It looks like when you tried to move your check-in date, another booking was called in, and it booted your reservation. There must have been a misstep on our end," Alexis said, tugging at the neck of her maroon turtleneck sweater. Her facial expressions went from frustrated and confused to repentant.

"I don't know how this could have happened. I'm truly, truly sorry." She stood firmly behind the small L-shaped counter that served as the "front desk," clicking and scrolling feverishly as if the results might magically change with enough refreshing. Small red and white poinsettias sat next to her laptop blaring the Temptations' harmonious rendition of "Silent Night."

Usually the song's soulful introduction and Dennis Edwards' *"In my mind,"* caused all the warmth and joy of Christmas to swell inside me. The only thing *in my mind* was how this was shaping up to be one of the worst Christmases ever.

"I promise you, we never, ever double-book. All this technology stuff is a mess." She rested her right palm across the embroidered "Aurbor Grove Inn" logo and tagline: *Our home is your home.*

"Well, can I speak to a manager or something?"

"I'm the co-owner."

I took a deep breath to calm my nerves, the light scent of pine mingled with apple cinnamon permeated throughout the house. Colorful lights rung around a lush green Christmas tree blinked steadily, the bright glare reflecting off large silver and gold ornaments. Large ivory and gold stockings dangled from the shelf above the unlit fireplace. The atmosphere had all the makings of a perfect holiday scene, which is why I'd wanted to stay there. But based on this news, instead of the dream Christmas I'd envisioned, I was living out a Halloween nightmare.

I would have to stay with Mama and endure her dating advice and complaints.

"And there's nothing you can do?" I asked.

"Unfortunately, we do not have any rooms available. Again, I am so sorry."

"What do I look like, Mary at the manger? There's no room for me at the inn?" I delivered the line with a straight face, but Alexis uncontrollably snorted a laugh.

"It ain't funny."

"Mrs. Brooks, I didn't mean —"

"Ms. It's just Ms."

"*Ms.* Brooks, I'm sorry. It's just the way," Alexis stopped short, pressing a palm to her chest. She raised a finger to her lip, attempting to suppress another laugh, then tried to recover, "I'm not laughing at you. I'm laughing with you. It's just when you said, Mary in a manger at the inn. This is the Inn. The visual got to me."

"I know what I said."

I didn't mean to do it, but the loudest, angriest growl escaped my lips as Eddie Kendrick's falsetto sang of sleeping in heavenly peace. It sounded like a noise a petulant child would make during a temper tantrum; the only thing missing was stamping my feet.

Alexis' face contorted with uncertainty on how to handle my mini meltdown. She opened her mouth to say something but clamped it shut at the rumble of someone jogging downstairs. The man stopped when he made it to the third step from the bottom, rubbing his hands together.

"Jasmine." He said my name slowly, his thick eyebrows knitting together, shock in his eyes. Then he showed off every one of his perfect white teeth. "This is crazy. You're *here.*"

"You?" I whispered with more disdain and less of the welcoming tone he offered me.

I knew Nell and her family had two rooms, but when Alexis mentioned that a special guest had bought out the rest of the rooms, including mine, I never would have guessed it was Kendall James, my ex, who had ignored me for 15 years.

All of a sudden, the bags and boxes I'd attempted to balance on my hip wobbled. The gift bags, door prizes, and carefully sorted decorations tumbled to the floor.

Alexis, with tight, curly tresses and an even tighter, nervous smile, squeaked as if anticipating the crash.

Out of time, energy, and patience, I just let it all fall. It was too much to carry in the first place.

Kendall rushed over to catch what he could. He saved the cardboard box packed with customized name tags, neatly stacking the items on the counter. With him came the scent of amber and cedar wood, the combination surprisingly made my stomach swirl...in a good way. Kendall smelled like a *grown man*, not the young guy I once cherished.

He reached out to hug me with one arm, but all I had was a mean "I can't believe this guy" glare. Finally relenting, I folded into his embrace, a place that was equally warm and comforting like it'd been all those years before we separated — like I was always meant to be right there. He held on for longer than I expected, so I pulled away first.

"I thought that sounded like a familiar voice," Kendall smiled, looking down on me with friendly brown eyes framed with long lashes. The twinkle in his irises, the way he bit his bottom lip, and stayed closer to me than necessary...

I took another step back.

It felt like decades instead of just one had passed, but he hadn't aged much. He still kept his jet-black hair low and wavy. He'd gained a thick black beard and a few pounds of muscle that were visible beyond the cream Ralph Lauren sweater hugging his frame.

How long had it been since I saw him in person? Was it graduation night? Oh yes. That was when I'd planned to talk to him about what would be next for us as we spent our last summer together before college. But he stood me up to head off to Atlanta and never returned home.

Before then, we had been so close. We both proudly resisted 'labels,' but everybody knew we were together. Knowing that we'd be apart, I desperately needed clarity. Privately, Kendall was always doing "boyfriend" things, yet sometimes called me his friend in front of people.

Then during senior year, he bailed on me so many times, always choosing music over me and everybody else. I always joked that chick Music was his first love. There was always some reason or excuse. Instead of hanging out, he had to practice. A showcase at a club in Atlanta took precedence over prom night, so I went with corny PJ Reece, who then proceeded to ruin my reputation by claiming we got a hotel room together.

The rumors not only had me looking crazy, but Mama interrogated me for days. None of that would have happened if Kendall had taken me like planned. He refused to apologize, and I couldn't let it go. We slowly but surely grew further apart, and any hopes of reconnecting over the summer evaporated.

Instead of a summer of love and fun, I'd grinded out the couple of months, working to save up money for college expenses without so much as a word from Kendall James.

It became obvious that his true love, over everything and everybody, especially me, was music. It seemed to have paid off. He was the classmate who 'made it' just like he said he would.

Since elementary school, Kendall was more than talented at singing, writing, and playing piano, drums, and guitar. He could ting a triangle, and have people dancing along. He topped every possible talent show or competition. His charm won him the right attention and a pass for average grades.

It'd never been a farfetched fantasy to him or many of our family and classmates. Still, everyone knew, at the end of the day, he was a country boy from South Georgia, and the odds would be against him. Forgoing college or work, he remained 100% committed to becoming the next R&B sensation.

Two years after high school, while hitting the dance floor with my classmates at Savannah College of Art and Design, affectionately called SCAD, the DJ announced a 'new hit'. He enthusiastically called the artist KJ the Great, but I instantly recognized the velvety voice that could quickly skip from a soulful tenor to a smooth, pitch-perfect falsetto.

I and millions of others would hear *"Forever Yours"* on repeat as part of the soundtrack for Will Smith's romantic comedy. The next thing I heard, he was on tour, opening for Usher.

Technically, me and Kendall were "friends" on social media, but that didn't count — he never liked anything I posted, wished me happy birthday or asked 'how's life treating you?' He constantly shared pictures, videos, and updates from his life of luxury, so I got to see plenty and piece together my own thoughts about him.

We likely had absolutely nothing in common anymore.

"Oh, so ya'll are friends?" Alexis piped up as if that made things better.

"You're the one who took my room?" I asked.

Fully confused, Kendall stammered, "I-I don't know what's going on."

"Ma'am, it's my fault. I mean, we are responsible for the error. What we can do, as a courtesy, is give one of our local hotels a call to see if —"

"They're all booked with people visiting for the Jingle Bell Festival, and most of the people attending the reunion are in our room blocks...except for this guy." I nodded toward Kendall with a scowl. "You're too good for the Laredo, huh?"

"I didn't even know about the room block. My assistant booked this place like we normally do." His eyes ran over me, and I felt another flash of heat. *What is going on? Settle down.*

I probably looked a mess, operating on less than four hours of sleep, one cup of coffee, no make-up, dressed in an old Aurbor Grove High hoodie and gray joggers that maybe, probably had paint stains.

"I'm still stuck on the fact that you rented *several* rooms. What did you do, bring a whole entourage to your class reunion? Why?"

"No, that's not it. Also, I just want to point out that you're here instead of the Laredo, too," he added, flashing a bright smile and raising his palm in a surrendering motion.

"Well, I personally booked this room so that I could set up everything for the class cocktail party tonight." I swiveled from Kendall to Alexis. "And now you're telling me I have nowhere to stay."

"Oh, uh," Kendall groaned. For a second, our eyes locked, and I felt that tingle again, so I looked back at Alexis' sympathetic glare.

Girl, get yourself together.

I felt him still eyeing me, so I found a dozen details to notice about the Aurbor Grove Inn entryway.

Were these original hardwood floors? And this rug — it's nice and thick. It had to cost at least $500. Hmm...chandelier... it looks like an antique.

"Look, you can have one of my rooms. Give her the Gardenia Room," he said, bringing my attention back to him.

"Oh, thank God," Alexis said, alongside a whoosh of relief. "I meant, I'll take care of it for you right away."

"But I booked the Tulip."

"But I've already put my things in the Tulip Room," Kendall said. "The Gardenia is the same size and has a better view."

"If it's the best, why aren't you staying there?" I countered.

Alexis looked between the two of us, the awkwardness palatable. "So..."

"You and I both know you do not want to be at your Mama's house. She'll take it," Kendall said. He winked at Alexis, but she didn't make a move until a few quiet seconds later, when I nodded in agreement.

"Okey-dokey, that worked out well, didn't it?"

I looked absently toward the dining room table outfitted with garland, silver-dusted pinecones, and red candles with electric, golden flames fluttering.

"You still living in Savannah, huh?"

"Yeah. I stayed there after college." I intentionally omitted the minor details that I racked up loads of debt, never graduated, and currently worked in banking instead of being the famous artist I thought I would be at this age.

I spent years of my childhood practicing my signature, only to end up using it to sign off on loan paperwork to help customers purchase homes and cars I couldn't afford, instead of canvases hanging in museums.

"I just need to switch a few more details in our system. Mr. James booked one night, and you wanted to stay through Christmas Day, correct?"

"Yes, that's right."

"Okay. We have a couple of guests coming in, so this will take some maneuvering to keep you in the same room your entire stay. Give me a minute."

"You really are home for Christmas, huh?" He winced at his own cheesy joke.

"Our family's doing a whole thing this year — both of my brothers and their families are coming down. I figured I'd be so tired after the class reunion festivities I'd need some time to recover in peace. You know how loud our house is."

"Your Mama could get up there, but your Dad was always the loudest," he chuckled. "It was like he was always in the pulpit and thought God couldn't hear good or something."

"Right. And it doesn't matter that they still act like I'm a child. Anyway, I decided to treat myself to a mini-vacation."

"In Aurbor Grove?"

"Listen, everybody can't be in Costa Rica for Christmas."

Kendall's eyes narrowed, and he smirked. "Hmmph. Interesting."

Crap! I let it slip that I'd been stalking his social media profile. *How else would I know he spent last Christmas frolicking in warm white sands and blue-green waters alongside a model.*

"Sorry, it's taking a while. Our internet is spotty," Alexis said.

"I mean, why did you book so many rooms?" I asked, squinting at him.

"You don't let anything go, do you?"

"I'm just saying, who does that?"

"Geez. I said you could have the room," Kendall said curtly. "You've got the room."

"Don't you think that's a little extra, though?"

"Drivers' license and credit card?" Alexis interrupted quietly. Without even glancing her way, I slid over my card and ID.

"You can still charge it to me," he said, pushing them back in my direction.

"The one night or the entire stay?" Alexis asked.

"I can pay my own way, you know."

"It's not a big deal. I'll take care of the whole stay. Consider it my Christmas gift." He picked up my card and handed it back to me, clasping it between my hands. "I got you."

"Whatever." Internally, I fought the offer but kept quiet. I wasn't crazy. I could barely afford the nightly rate that had pushed my credit card toward its limit in the first place. Here he was flaunting, like a thousand-plus dollars was nothing to him.

Must be nice. That's when it spilled out.

"I want you to know this. You may be a whole celebrity elsewhere," I began loudly, twirling my finger in a circle, "but around here, you're just Skinny Kenny James, Mrs. June's grandson."

He opened his mouth to offer a retort, then doubled over with laughter. His joy echoed throughout the foyer. It was contagious and eventually turned my frustrated frown into a giggle.

"I'm sorry. I...it's been a long day." Truthfully, it'd been a long life, and seeing Kendall brought back too many memories and missed dreams all at one time. I couldn't manage it all and maintain the front of happiness.

"It's only 1:30." He looked down at his Apple Watch to double-check.

I rolled my eyes. "Feels like it should be five o'clock and happy hour already. We've been planning this reunion forever, and this is not the start I imagined. Ramona and Nell should be here soon to help finish setting up, so I won't have any time to relax before we get to work."

"Look at our class officers fulfilling their civic duty."

"I guess," I mumbled. "*Your* classmates have gotten on my last nerve wanting all this fancy stuff but not wanting to pay more than $50 a ticket. And then we had dozens claim they would be willing to volunteer, but in the end, it's just us."

"That sounds like our class," he said. "Well, I'm here. I can help with whatever you need."

"Hmm, okay. I'll take you up on that. We'll need someone to help the DJ set up."

"Got it."

Alexis' playlist picked up its tempo, transitioning to Donnie Hathaway's "This Christmas." I couldn't help but move my head to the beat a little, and of course, Kendall began to sing along.

"This is the best Christmas song, isn't it?" He effortlessly belted out the chorus, sounding 99.9% like the original.

I shook my head, smiling, "Show off."

"Okay, you are all set. You can leave all of that here, and I can show you to your room," Alexis said.

"I'll help you with your luggage," Kendall offered.

"No, it's okay, I got it. Looks like you were headed out anyway, and I legit took up all of your time already."

"Just headed to see my grandma — you know, Mrs. June."

"I told you, I didn't mean anything by that. I'm tired. And hungry. Sorry for my Snickers commercial moment. I'll be nicer tonight, I promise. Thank you...for the room."

Alexis cleared her throat to catch my attention. "Right this way," she said, heading up the stairs.

"Let's get lunch then?"

"Ramona's on the way. Nell's at lunch with her family and will be back soon. I don't have time," I said over my shoulder, stomping up the stairs behind Alexis. "Tell Mrs. June I said hello."

I wanted to feel a spark of satisfaction, rejecting him, but instead, an ache panged on the inside, knowing we were parting ways. Funny, how a few minutes with this one guy activated something I thought was very much gone.

The front door closed as the two of us made it to the top of the stairs. Knowing that Kendall was gone-gone, I exhaled so deeply. Clearly, I didn't know what to do in his presence. I wanted to be mad and keep my distance, but this excitement kept bubbling up alongside a deep desire to be with him.

If the Lord made me be completely honest, Kendall was the one person I wanted to see most but also the one I suspected wouldn't make an appearance at the class reunion. Surely, he would be on the road somewhere or simply too good to head back to our small town to pretend like he was normal like the rest of us. I didn't dare check the RSVP list. Well, with the exception of ensuring PJ Reece wasn't coming.

"The Gardenia is actually better than the Tulip Room, if you asked me," Alexis said. "But you didn't ask me. I just want to make sure you know Mr. James did right by you."

"Mr. James?"

"I'm trying to be professional. Okay, girl, we used to call him Skinny Kenny too," Alexis said, stifling a laugh with a balled fist.

She opened up the room bearing a wreath with a red, velvet bow and two small golden bells that jingled. Bright sunlight washed over the plush white and cream bedding that reminded me of the room's namesake flower. I would definitely have to be careful with my pens, markers, and black coffee in this space.

"The Gardenia offers one of the best views of the gardens. It also has a private patio where you can enjoy a morning cup of coffee or tea. It's been unseasonably warm, but if it gets too chilly, you can wrap up in one of our luxury throws."

I followed Alexis to the sliding glass door, stepping outside. I took in the acres of naked winter trees alongside green shrubbery and blooms of a variety of shades of salmon, red, and bright pink. I wasn't into flowers, so I had no idea what I was looking at, but nevertheless, the view brought me peace.

"It's not quite as beautiful as it is in spring or summer, but still nice to look at, and my husband tries to make it look extra special with the Christmas decorations," Alexis said.

Candy canes dotted the pathways throughout the garden. White lights ringed around a pergola swing, and bright, colorful bulbs sparkled up and down a tall fir tree in the middle of the gardens. In the far east corner, I spotted an inflatable snowman towering over everything, at his feet were a group of reindeer gathered atop a pile of fake white snow. A mechanical Santa Claus stood toward the back, waving a hand and lightly greeting, "Ho, ho, ho."

As if reading my mind or simply following my eyes as they darted across the perfectly manicured grounds, Alexis said, "Don't worry, we kept most of the Christmas stuff on the perimeter and away from the private event space, so it won't clash with your decorations. Some people like it, though."

"It's nice," I said. "I've always wondered what it would be like to stay here. My bus used to pass this house all the time. I was a young, broke teen, and it all seemed so fancy."

"Well, you're here, now. Look at how much has changed."

I stared longingly at the beautiful landscape.

"Yeah. Not so much young anymore, but definitely still broke."

* * *

"When we ran for class officers, nobody told me that I'd have to do all this work for the rest of my life," Ramona mumbled, fixing one of the centerpieces on the highboy table.

We attached glossy pictures of students to a stick with Class of 2001 cut out in glittery gold, then placed them in mason jars, wrapped in twine and black ribbon.

"Got us out here like Supreme Court Justices — with a lifetime appointment," I said. "I just wanted something extra to put on my college application."

"Less talking, more setup," Nell quipped, breezing by with a hand truck with cases of wine. She pulled out bottles of white, red, and sparkling rose bottles, sitting them next to small black napkins with *A Holiday Reunion, December 23, 2016* scrawled on them in gold cursive.

"With everything else that went wrong today, I am pleasantly surprised how all of this has worked out," I said, flitting about, ensuring each glittery gold tablecloth fit perfectly.

"Maybe God wanted to give us a break. Earlier this week I had my own family drama happening, then Ramona almost lost her job. It's been a Christmas to remember," Nell said, scratching the sleek edge of her ponytail.

"Ramona, you didn't mention that."

"I am still thinking through it all myself. Let's just say my kids showed up and showed out for me."

"Well, I'm glad we'll give classmates an opportunity to donate to YEC tonight," I said.

"We need every dollar, dime we can get."

"Oh, that reminds me, we need to get some cash out of the account in case somebody decides to show up and pay tonight," I said.

"I don't think we should let them in."

"*Nell.* Now you know we can't do that — and I bet I'd catch all the heat. I can hear it now: Jasm*ean* wouldn't even let me in."

"Well, I just hope we actually get to enjoy this and catch up with each other. For the past six months, all we talk about is the class reunion this and the class reunion that," Ramona said, rolling her eyes.

Nell picked up the box of plastic name tags and neatly organized them in alphabetical order on a six-foot table near the entrance of the gardens.

"Why did we get name tags? Everybody knows everybody," she said.

"I mean...as the one who still lives here," Ramona began, "trust me when I say everybody doesn't look the same. There are some people I see at Walmart who yell, 'hey classmate,' and I have zero idea who it is."

"Ramona. Stop it. Right now," Nell hushed.

"It's true. I mean I know I look different. I know I'm extra fluffy these days."

"I'd like to believe that we've all aged like fine wine," I said, pausing to pose with a hand on my hip.

"Some of us look more like Boone's Farm," Ramona chuckled. "Well, I know one thing, I vote that our 20th is during the summer."

She wrapped her black and white checkered scarf around her neck.

"C'mon it's not *that* cold. With the tent and heat lamps, it will be nice," I said.

"December is the only time a bunch of out-of-towners come home to Aurbor Grove," Nell muttered. "It's nice because the semester is over so you're not getting run over by the college kids. A lot of folks still like to attend the Jingle Bell Festival. Bella has loved every bit of being here. I overheard her talking to Emery about moving. He put a stop to that real quick."

"There is a difference between visiting and living here," Ramona said, picking up the iPad to review the RSVPs. "Well, we're up to 75 people, including spouses, and dates and stuff. Okay, this might be a nice affair."

"I knew a lot of people would buy tickets at the last minute," I said.

"Hold up. Wait a minute." With wide eyes, Ramona dramatically flipped her black bang with her index finger and huddled next to Nell.

Fearful of what went wrong, I jogged over to them to look at the iPad screen.

"What are we looking at here?" Nell asked, confused.

Ramona plopped a finger on the screen. "Why didn't anybody tell me that *the* Kendall James aka KJ the Great was going to be here?"

"Oh girl, bye." Nell rolled her eyes. "I knew it, but I don't think we should create a whole scene."

Nell moved on to setting up the memorial table featuring candles and framed images of classmates who'd passed too soon.

That was my cue to act occupied too, slinking away to fix a table that was perfectly fine. Everything was practically complete, and thoughts of Kendall returned—our hug, his smile, the lingering questions I never got to ask years ago.

I'd been so busy that he hadn't crossed my mind...much. Now Ramona was forcing me to remember. To remember the way he looked at me, a strange mix of familiarity and longing. To remember how his voice sent shock waves all the way to my heart. To remember how comfortable it was to be with him again.

"Dang it. He has a plus one." That piece of information made me stop fiddling with the centerpiece, which happened to be a group shot, including me and Kendall hugged up after our performance in the high school musical *"Annie."* He'd played the scoundrel Rooster alongside my scheming Lily St. Regis character. Our "Easy Street" performance had us singing in harmony and earned more rave reviews than the more popular "Tomorrow" tune sung by Annie.

God, I couldn't escape him!

"Do you think we can get him to perform a few songs? *Forever Yours* is my song," Ramona said.

"It's a'ight," I muttered. "He sounds too much like a knockoff Anthony Hamilton if you asked me."

"Okay, hater," Nell said.

"I'm not hating. I'm just saying, it's obvious he's trying hard to prove something in that song."

"Well, whatever he did, it worked its magic on me and my husband," Ramona said, swirling her hips. "We played it at our wedding."

"Jasmine, why don't you ask Skinny Kenny to sing us a tune. Y'all still cool, right?" Nell said.

"What happened to us not making a scene? Now you're trying to turn the man into a headliner for our class reunion."

"Uh-unh, what is up with you?" Ramona muttered. "You got beef with Kendall or something?"

"Oh, uh, no. I don't know. Don't y'all feel like he acts like he's better than us?"

Nell shook her head 'no' at the same time Ramona said, "He is better than us."

I scoffed. "You're acting like a whole fan right now."

"Look, I am a fan, but it's the truth. This man is doing what he loves, living his dream life — I know 'cause I follow him online. He could be with whoever he wants in the world and buy whatever he wants when he wants." Ramona paused, hunching her shoulders up to the white feather earrings dangling from her lobes. "None of us can do any of that. Shoot, maybe I should ask him for a donation to YEC."

"That doesn't give him the right to treat us like we're less than. Money isn't everything. I mean —"

"This is looking good ladies," a deep voice bellowed, interrupting my rebuttal. Arms outstretched, with a large brown bag in hand, Kendall sauntered down the steps, towards us in the garden.

"Of course, he has to make an entrance," I mumbled, touching my pounding temple. "You're early for your assignment. DJ doesn't arrive until 7."

"What's up Skinny Kenny?" Ramona practically ran to him and forced a bear hug that clearly made him uncomfortable. "Hmm, you ain't so skinny anymore, I feel. I mean, I see." She rested her palm on the center of his chest, smiling and looking up at him.

"Can I take a selfie?" She whipped out her phone and took the snap before he could say yes or even pose. "Oops, let's do that again. Look at the camera this time. And smile like we know each other. But don't make my husband mad."

"Hey, Nell," he said, untangling himself from Ramona.

"Hey Skinny Kenny!" She threw up the peace sign and continued to organize props for the photo booth.

"Jasmine," he began, "I got something for you to eat."

Ramona made a face as if to say, *"Okay, Skinny Kenny, I see you."* I could imagine it because I'd seen the face and heard her say that very phrase a few times throughout our high school years.

I wanted to brush him off, but my stomach immediately betrayed me, wailing loudly for sustenance.

"We can sit in the dining room and catch up," he said, hope in his voice.

"Yeah, go 'head girl, we're about to leave anyway," Ramona added to eliminate her last excuse for declining his offer. "I already set up the stations, but I'll be back to meet the caterer and go over everything."

Nell piled on. "After I finish with this, we're good to go. I got the projector ready to roll the slide show. That gives us a few hours until everybody starts showing up? Plenty of time to *catch up.*"

"See you later." Ramona fanned her shimmering pearlescent stiletto fingertips as if to push me in Kendall's direction.

"It's just a late lunch," he said with a shrug. "You'll have plenty of room for hors d'oeuvres later."

I did not want to be close to him again, and I definitely didn't want to be alone. *What would they talk about? Who was his plus one?*

He held out his hand to lead me up the steps, and I accepted even though there was little risk of me stumbling in my sneakers.

Once I was seated, Kendall lifted a styrofoam plate from the bag and sat it in front of me.

"I figured you hadn't had this in a while."

Before he could open the top, I already knew: The Que.

"You didn't."

"I did."

"Ribs?"

"Yep — dry rubbed with Ike's special spicy barbecue sauce on the side for dipping."

"Smoked wings?"

"Flats only with ranch dressing."

"Mac and cheese?"

"With a burnt edge."

"Pulled pork?"

"Pulled chicken 'cause you tryin' to be a lil' healthy."

I howled, laughing at his perfect recitation of my order from back in the day. I could not stop smiling, as well fell into our usual rhythm of knowing what the other required, even something as simple as a meal.

"This right here is going to hit the spot so good. I was hungry earlier, but dealing with Ramona and Nell kept me so busy I forgot to eat." I took a bite out of the sweet, square of golden cornbread before anything else.

"Ma'am, can we say the blessing first? Pastor Brooks would be ashamed."

Wiping crumbs from my mouth, I placed my hands in his and closed my eyes.

"Dear God, thank you for this delicious meal. We pray that it be a blessing and nourishment for our bodies. We also thank you for bringing us back together again, and we trust that you will continue to guide and strengthen us. God, please watch over us and our classmates as they make their way here. Amen."

"I see you still praying those good, old-school Baptist blessings."

"You can take the boy out of the country, but you can't take the country out of the boy."

Ripping apart the rib, I waved a bone at him. "You lied to me."

"Wait, what?"

"You told me I'd have room for hors d'oeuvres. I am eating all of this. *All-of-it,* you hear me?"

We thoroughly enjoyed every greasy, saucy, messy bite of our food, reminiscing on our school days in between.

"I told you not to go into Mr. Lassiter's class."

"I thought he liked me."

"Mr. Lassiter didn't like anybody."

"As soon as I walked up in there, he sent me straight to the office. 'Mr. James, you should know better,'" Kendall said, mimicking their teacher's nasally voice.

As the laughter died down, I let go of a very satisfied sigh. Nothing like good food and good company to lift your spirit.

"Thank you for this. For everything."

My phone dinged, alerting me to a message from Ramona. *"Hey...dj won't be able to make it. His daughter's sick."*

"Welp, you don't have to worry about helping the DJ. He's not coming." I quickly thumbed in a reply with lots of angry emojis. "That's what I get for booking Ramona's second cousin on her Daddy's side."

"Dang, I'm sorry to hear that," Kendall said.

"I knew a few things would go wrong, but how can you have a party without a DJ?"

"That's a quick fix, though — we can hook up some speakers, and somebody can stream the music."

"People paid for this. I wanted it to feel more special, I guess."

"The special part is in us reuniting."

Us. I wondered if he meant 'us' as in the whole class or the two of us.

I took another spoonful of my Mac and cheese even though I was beyond full.

"The Inn does events like this all the time. I'll talk to Alexis and see if they have speakers on hand. If not, I can go to the store and see what they have," Kendall said. He turned to find Alexis, then paused and faced me again, grabbing my hands. Like he often did when we were teenagers, he circled his thumbs across my skin. The gentle touch, soothing and calming. "It's going to work out fine."

And just like back then, I believed him. That ability to trust and to lean on someone — I missed that. I missed Kendall.

A few minutes later, he came back wearing a half-cringe-half smile. At his side was a small, silver karaoke machine. "This is the best she could do."

"Okay. Okay. We can say we're doing karaoke and pretend like it was part of the plan all along? Maybe we can pull up songs and lyrics on the projector."

"Look at you, Miss Class Vice President. Always figuring out a silver lining."

Proud of my quick solution, I smiled, then dusted off my shoulder. "I try."

"Let's make sure this thing works." He fumbled with the plug, searching for a wall socket. With the microphone in hand, he looked like the singer he was, and the thought tumbled out of my mouth before I had a chance to filter it.

"I miss hearing your voice."

"I miss singing for you." Kendall cast a furtive glance her way.

"When are you coming out with something new?"

"I actually dropped a Christmas single a few weeks ago. It hasn't quite caught on like I thought it would," he said, disappointment in his voice. "It's hard to do Christmas music. Everybody likes the classics. And I get it. There's a comfort there. Besides, you never know when your time is up in this business."

"You are not done. Your voice, your words, they mean something to people. You...mean a lot to some of us."

I could visibly see how my affirmation and confession strengthened him. He went from slumped shoulders and nibbling on the inside of his jaw to standing tall and smiling again.

"You want to hear it?"

"Of course. I don't know how I missed it in the first place. I always try to catch all your songs."

Okay, relax, now you're admitting too much.

I watched him slide his thumb up his phone screen, tap, tap, tap to connect it to the karaoke machine's Bluetooth.

A soft piano melody filled the dining room, then his voice. It started just as quietly as the keys, steadily expanding in volume and passion.

That voice...

I could tell by the way he monitored my reaction, he wanted me to like it.

"This sounds beautiful."

"It's better if you dance to it."

He reached out and pulled me up to him. Towering almost six inches over my head, he gripped my waist as we moved slowly from side to side stiffly.

He hugged me, his breath dancing across my skin, "I'm glad *you* like it. It's about you."

Too embarrassed to look him in the eye, I searched for a distraction — anything, anybody.

"Hmmph. It's almost time, and I have got to get ready. I can hear Ramona complaining if she sees me still dressed in these clothes."

That gave us a good reason to separate, but for some reason, I didn't move too far. Neither did he.

"Can you stay a little longer? I may never have another chance to have you to myself tonight."

"Oh, cause everybody's going to be clamoring for your autograph?"

"No. Because..."

His words hung in the air, the sound of his own voice crooning about finding true love during Christmas in the background. His mouth moved, but he hesitated.

"What is it?"

"I'm gonna just say it. I've always felt like we could have been more. We should have been more."

I averted my eyes, pulling away. He lightly touched my chin, raising it.

"I don't know what happened between us back then. I apologize for not showing up for you. I understand if you can't forgive me for back then, but I can't help but think, what about now? What if we tried again? Like really tried."

"Kendall." All I could say was his name. I had wondered the same thing over the years, but considered it foolish to imagine a happily ever after of my own.

I never finished my degree, settling for a job at the bank. While I was proud that I'd worked my way up from teller to loan officer, it still didn't compare to singing on stage at Madison Square Garden. Images of him on the beach with that model flashed in my mind's eye.

Ramona's voice echoed in my ears, *"Dang it. He has a plus one."*

Suddenly I became even more self-conscious about my funk from bustling all day, the oversized hoodie stained with barbecue sauce and my kinky, curly hair that'd ballooned into a messy afro. I took a step back, but he held onto my hands, refusing to let go.

"We are in two different places. We're not kids anymore. You have an amazing career and life. I have...my own thing. After tonight, you're going to go back to whatever awesome location, and I'll be back in Savannah. I think you're just getting caught up in--in the nostalgia."

"No. I'm remembering what's real," he said. "Don't get me wrong, I love music. That's real. I hate the entertainment business. That's so fake. This time with you—that's the realest I've been able to be since I don't know when. You don't let me get caught up in my ego."

"I did kinda check you."

"More than once," he said. "If you say it's beautiful, I know you mean it."

"Despite the distance and the time, I still care about you. I have no reason to lie to you. "

"I missed that," he said. "Part of why I bought so many rooms here was I didn't want to run into anybody, faking it and pretending all the time. I just wanted to be...normal. My assistant wanted to come to keep me company and make sure I didn't look lame attending my class reunion solo. My publicist said it could affect my image or whatever, but I told her not to come. All of that's just silly."

So that was his plus one?

"I guess I hadn't thought of all that — the cons of being rich and famous."

"Don't get me wrong. I am blessed. More than blessed, and I thank God for it, but I'm like you — I wanted some quiet time before I have to go out and play Mr. Perfect.

"I thought I wanted to be alone, but what I really wanted was peace. When you showed up, I remembered what that felt like," he said. "What it felt like to be me. To simply be, what did you call me again? Mrs. June's grandson?"

"I'm never going to live that down, am I?"

"Nope." He shook his head, smiling. "I don't want to go back to what it was like before. I know what I want. Do you?"

His eyes serious, he didn't even blink, he waited patiently for an answer.

The room went silent as the app randomly selected Kendall's next song, an uptempo collaboration with a rapper.

"I do. I mean, at least I think I might. This is a little crazy though, right?" I waved my hand in the air. "Hours ago, I was dang near cussing you out and now...what do we even call this?"

"We're catching up."

"Oh, it's that simple?"

"Yes."

"Well, what do we do next?"

"You're going to be my date for my high school reunion," he said matter-of-factly.

"Okay." How this all was made my heart and stomach flutter. Maybe I wouldn't go empty-armed to the class reunion after all.

"Do you think I wanted to come to see my classmates that bad? I see them online, all in my inbox, asking for autographs and trying to get me to do free shows."

"Wait, what?" I cackled.

"Yes. Your girl Ramona has been DM-ing me about doing her wedding anniversary every year."

"She is too much."

"I didn't come back to kick it with them — I came back for you. I had to try."

"This is a lot to think about."

"Don't think then. You're so smart already. With that forehead, you should already know everything. "

I slapped his shoulder, shaking my head.

"Look, all jokes aside, I don't want you to feel like you have to make a decision or change anything. I'm not asking you to marry me. I'm asking you to go out on a date. One date."

"One date?"

He nodded his head slowly, touching hers. "And maybe I

can stay through Christmas Day too?"

As if on cue, Spotify skipped to Kendall's next song, the hit that started it all: *Forever Yours.*

He didn't speak, allowing the song to say everything that needed to be said.

Maybe as some defense mechanism, I had intentionally blocked out the lyrics to the song all this time because I didn't want to fantasize that he was talking about me. I didn't want to play the "Is he into me or not?" guessing game knowing we couldn't be together. Most of his actions had convinced me he was not. Yet, in one day, he had gone above and beyond to prove otherwise.

Kendall closed his eyes briefly as he sang along, climbing to hit the high note. In that instant, I realized all along he was telling a story about them — of what was and what could have been.

Now I had a chance to find out.

He lilted the words that made me feel like I was floating and no one else existed in my world except him. Our world.

He opened his eyes, vocalizing a promise that had withstood 15 years.

"And that's why I want you to know, that I am forever yours."

Inching forward, he pressed his lips against mine, wrapping his arms tighter and holding me so close. We separated only for a split second to confirm if we both felt the same magic.

"You are something else," I said, laughing.

He laughed too, then kissed me once again on the forehead. "*This* is the reunion I've been planning for a long time."

I rested my head on his shoulder, closed my eyes, and wondered: *what would it be like if it was like this forever?*

"I cannot believe this." At that moment, I thought, maybe, just maybe, this was all meant to be.

Epilogue

December 25, 2016

It was the morning of Christmas, when all throughout the house, no person, spirit, trouble, or martini stirred, not even the bed and breakfast owner's spouse. Her hand-stitched, empty stockings hung by the chimney with care, in hopes that somebody, anybody might see fit to drop a gift or two in there. The guy I liked was still nestled all snug in his bed, while visions of our future together danced in my head.

Maybe I'd been bitten by the artist bug again, but when I arose before the sun on Christmas Day, I had words on my mind that I wanted to write down.

I curled up on the sofa in the living room, watching the lights on the Christmas tree dance. Warmth and fake crackling noises emanated from the electric fireplace. I let the throw fall from my shoulders as I sipped coffee.

It hadn't been the Christmas I'd plotted and planned in my mind, but it was so much more. What was I going to do with all of this?

The past few days with Kendall by my side completely exceeded every fairytale I watched or read, because it was *mine.* It's not like we did anything extraordinary or grand — we talked, ate, laughed, sang, and danced.

We continued to "catch up."

That phrase had a double meaning for me now. It wasn't just a matter of us dumping out all the updates about our lives.

I realized it wasn't a competition or about him being better or ahead of me, or me feeling like I was behind.

We were finding our beat with every conversation and every moment together. And on this Christmas Day, we were moving at the same tempo. It was our time. That's what a 'second chance' gave us, and I didn't have to count myself a fool for considering it.

My phone dinged as the text message popped up, interrupting my deep thoughts.

> Ramona: Merry Christmas everybody. We decided to hit the beach! I'm on vacation. Like a real vacation.

Of course, Ramona had to be first to deliver holiday greetings. Shortly after, a swooping sound came through as a picture of her in a two-piece, in all her beautiful fluffiness, holding hands with Mark as the sun rose.

> Jasmine: Friend, I'm so happy for you. Merry Christmas! Love you.

Nell: Merry Christmas! We're still waking up. See you at church,

Jasmine. Have fun, Ramona!

"What are you doing up at the crack of dawn? Literally."

His voice startled me. I turned to see Kendall dressed in workout clothes, his phone in hand, earbuds stuffed in his ears.

"Just wanted to soak in the goodness of this Christmas morning before I have to go to church. I can't have my Mama fussing at me all day."

"I'm about to go for a run, but now you have me thinking otherwise."

"No, go. Do your thing."

"I don't think you get it. I got you back in my life, and every moment I can have, I will take. We are about to sit right here together, sipping coffee, laughing, and enjoying each other's company."

"That does sound nice."

"Oh, it's happening." Kendall joined me on the couch. I set my journal aside. I wrapped my arms around his neck, as he rested his head on my chest and kicked his feet up.

"I was thinking. What if we went out on another date, then a few more, and then spent New Year's Eve together."

"That might could work," I said. "But if you really want to impress me — how about you go to church with me? That'll get my Mama to stop asking me about my dating life. Did you bring any 'church clothes?'"

"Does your Mama even like me?"

"Eh, you're a'ight. If she googles your performances, she might start asking me double questions."

"Just remind her I'm Mrs. June's grandson. That should get me some cool points."

Author's Note

Merry Christmas!! Thank you so much for joining me in a quick visit to Aurbor Grove during the holidays. I hope these stories warmed your heart and brought hope, humor, and happy endings that made you smile.

Part of me wants more from this place and people, but I've had to settle for a little taste in these three short stories. At least for now. Early drafts of this were way more complicated. I may share these with my VIP list so be sure you're signed up at www.LakeshiaPoole.com.

I wanted to give people something they could sit down and sip on for an hour. Our schedules are so jam-packed, and we're so busy, an hour to get away to another fictional place where people reunite, messes get cleaned up, and love finds its way home is a luxury.

I do not take it for granted that you chose to spend that hour with me, Nell, Jasmine, and Ramona. *Thank you.* I love Christmas stories — I don't care how corny, cheesy, predictable, or fantastical they can be, I need them in my life. I was in the middle of working on a book project that's not quite as light and writing these stories gave me a much needed reprieve.

When you live in a society where there's always something negative leading the headlines, we're on the brink of some destruction — politically, economically, environmentally—or you personally experience trial after trial, it's nice to escape.

I like to go to a place where things always work out. That predictability is soothing and comforting.

In *A Holiday Reunion*, I didn't want to ignore the real world completely but to give a glimpse of what's possible when we take a moment to try out love — loving ourselves and loving others. Love is potent. I don't want us ever to downplay what's possible when we lead with love. When we give others a second chance, we open the door for love to lead the way.

Whatever you're going through right now, I hope *A Holiday Reunion* sparked your imagination to see how love might help you get through.

You probably noticed that in each story, my main characters' top obstacle wasn't external forces, but internal wounds. To get through to the other side, they had to admit something about themselves to themselves. Self-awareness is key when you're on a journey of healing. It doesn't mean that surrounding circumstances are fair or that they don't affect us; what it means is we all have *stuff* we need to take a look at and ask if it's serving us or is it holding us back?

We've built habits and walls to protect ourselves, but those same walls shut out people and resources that are meant to help us. How can we establish better boundaries or a stronger sense of self to live a life that serves us (and others) well? It doesn't mean that at the snap of a finger, everything will be alright. It doesn't mean we shouldn't hold people accountable for the pain they cause. Self-inventory and self-mastery are only parts of the puzzle, but truly they are the only ones we have control over.

I also wanted to show how, no matter the plans we set for ourselves, even when we fall short in our eyes, God's grand plan is still at work. There's nothing you can do so amazing or terrible to ruin God's plans. You are loved. You are needed. You are a blessing. Don't ever forget that!

Lakeshia

Happily Ever Christmas

About Happily Ever Christmas

Tragedy brings her home. Love just might make her stay.

Christmas is Ebony's least favorite time of year. She's no Scrooge, but the season sparks painful memories. Instead of her usual ritual of working feverishly through the holidays, an emergency pulls her back home. Forced to help with the family bed and breakfast and stay for the Annual Jingle Bell Festival, Ebony reconnects with family and a long lost love. Healing past wounds, enjoying present moments, and opening up to future possibilities isn't easy, but Ebony's journey home this Christmas may very well lead to her happily ever after. This is a sweet, clean story about family and enduring love. If you're a fan of Hallmark and Lifetime feel-good holiday movies, curl up and read Happily Ever Christmas.

Chapter One

"Merry Christmas to you too."

I didn't mean it. But I had to say it to get my client off the phone.

You have to repeat the phrase all of December. Otherwise, people would swear you were a heartless Scrooge.

"That was the driest Merry Christmas I ever heard," my coworker Samantha said, pointing her pen at me. "You sounded like a kid who didn't get anything she wanted under the tree."

"We don't have time for all the pleasantries." I ran my fingers down the bone-straight ends of my hair. I was still getting used to the silky tresses instead of my thick, tight curls. My hairstylist called it the Anna Wintour bob and said the style made me look like a boss. *Whatever.*

I rarely straightened my hair, and I missed twirling the ends when I got stressed.

"I didn't think they'd ever stop talking about their Christmas plans, and let us actually get to work."

My laptop dinged, alerting me that only 10% of the

battery remained. That's about how much energy I felt like I had left.

What was supposed to be a 30-minute call recapping the product launch event for our client, Thin Quick, had turned into a two-hour brainstorm.

Samantha and I huddled in the comfy crème leather chairs in the sitting area of my office. Sunlight poured in through the floor-to-ceiling windows shining a natural spotlight on the yellow sticky notes and stacks of file folders covering the round table between us.

I promise there was a method to our messy madness. Corporations like Thin Quick turned to our public relations firm to bring their products and brands to life and to the masses. The fancy word we used to sell these services was experiential marketing. But it all boiled down to coordinating large-scale events that attracted a lot of attention, positive press, and sales.

"Well, at least the Thin Quick people are happy," Samantha said. "It's not every day you hear praise like that from your largest client."

"They're so pleased, they gave us extra work. *Yay.*"

With everyone resolving to lose a few pounds, December and January were the biggest sales periods for Thin Quick. After a successful Los Angeles event and PR launch, they wanted us to replicate the same type of campaign in New York —in less than a month.

"But, extra work means we can ask for extra budget." Samantha rubbed invisible money between her fingertips, raising an eyebrow.

"And around here, extra budget makes everybody happy," I laughed.

More funds to close out the year would certainly make our firm's Managing Director Paula *extra* happy. Paula had all but promised to bump me up to my dream title of Vice President if I continued to bring in new business. Expanding the Thin Quick account by another $100K would earn me the promotion I deserved.

Finally, all of the 14-hour days, restless nights, traveling last minute from city-to-city would pay off!

"Make sure you send the final report from the launch event to Paula too. Include all the social media analytics too — she'll love the fact that the Thin Quick shake was the #1 trending topic. I'll update her on the new proposal and budget."

I typed and talked fast, chomping off half a cinnamon-raisin bagel. Even though it approached 2:30 pm, I hadn't finished breakfast yet. Bitter and black coffee wasn't ideal at room temperature, but I gulped down the much-needed caffeine anyway.

Samantha ticked off all of the ideas the client had thrown out during our call. A lot of them weren't viable on such a short timeline in the midst of the holidays, but we always aimed to make it happen.

We were halfway through brainstorming alternative ideas for the new proposal when my laptop's screen went black.

Oh, shoot! I knew better, but I pressed the power button repeatedly, hoping it would come back on.

"If we do something like 'New Year in New York,' we can get a celebrity party host and serve the shakes in little shot glasses. Or maybe a celebrity trainer would be better?" Samantha asked.

As I was about to answer, the phone rang, lighting up red.

I picked up on the second ring. "This is Ebony."

"It's Kim. I have your sister Alexis on line 1. She says it's an emergency."

I could only imagine what my drama queen sister-*in-law* Alexis wanted. Something was always going on with my older brother Manny and his wife.

Nine-times out of 10, their problem was financial. I'd set up a special checking account for them to keep these 'emergency calls' to a minimum.

"Tell her I'll call her back after my meeting." I pressed the speakerphone button OFF to return to my discussion with Samantha.

"Where was I? I like the idea of a host, but I don't think a trainer will get us the attention we want."

"I guess it is the same as what everybody else does."

"Right. And we don't want people to think of Thin Quick as the usual 'diet.' It's a lifestyle brand."

The muted television I kept on to stay on the pulse of breaking news caught my attention. The gorgeous singer Lourdés Michele threw her head back in laughter. She looked like a modern-day Marilyn Monroe but with fire-red hair instead of blond.

Known more for her provocative selfies, swimsuit photoshoots, and Hollywood romances than hit songs, Lourdés was the 'it' celebrity of the moment.

"I want to make her the new face of Thin Quick."

Samantha twisted in her chair to get a good look at the screen. "Okay. She is definitely something different."

"We may have to prep her for media interviews, but she loves the camera. And it loves her right back. Usually, TV makes you look bigger, but she is perfect on-screen," I said.

"She's almost too good to be true." Samantha's chair squished as she shifted, crossing her legs. "I can see why Thin Quick would want her as a spokesperson. I think their customers wish they had a body like hers, but does this approach feel a little too perfect?"

"There's no such thing as too perfect. We have to sell people on what they think they want. Even if it's a little unrealistic."

"I know I'd buy a truckload of Thin Quick meals if I

believed they could make me look like Lourdés," Samantha muttered.

"Exactly! So, if you could work with legal to draft a contract that we can send over for the client to review along with the proposal, that'll help keep everything moving."

I walked over to my desktop computer. It chimed at the arrival of a new message at the same time my cell phone buzzed.

Alexis' number and picture popped up on the screen—it was a photo of her playing air guitar in front of the Elvis statue in Memphis. I tapped IGNORE to silence the call and pulled up my e-mail inbox.

Click.

Scroll.

Delete.

Happy Holidays and out-of-office e-mails crowded out important messages from clients and staff. I wished I could automatically send the end of year notes to the trash. Scratch that, I wished I could toss the whole of December and return to business as usual.

I clicked through the Thin Quick files until I found a collage of images, showcasing before and after pictures of real Thin Quick customers. Short, tall. Pear-shaped. Narrow as a 2x4 beam. A cross-section of ethnicities and ages. All of these women had stories, either wanting to lose or gain a few pounds. Some battled weight challenges since childhood, and others faced health crises that nearly stole their lives. They overcame incredible odds, not to be skinny, but to be healthier and happier.

I attached the photos and testimonies that tugged at the heart to a new e-mail message for Samantha. "I'm sending you some photos and customer reviews I want featured on the campaign website."

Samantha scooted to the edge of the chair, laptop wobbling on her knees.

"We discussed quite a lot today. The new proposal, contracts, and I'll have to do some research for our budget. You want the website updated today too?"

My eyes glued to the computer monitor, I flashed a smile. "That would be perfect!"

"I was hoping to leave a little early, so I could make the office Christmas party." Her voice was as strained as the smile plastered on her face.

Having worked with Samantha for over six years, I noticed she did this thing when she didn't agree with someone, stretching out the end of words into a sing-song. It reminded me of how moms talked to their children when they refused to share or take turns on the playground slide.

"If you've been to one office Christmas party, haven't you been to them all?" I asked, shrugging.

"Well, I won't be able to stay long because I have to catch a flight home for the holidays."

"You're taking off this early?" I paused to look at the calendar, counting the time left before Christmas with the oval tip of my nude-colored pinky nail – 12 days.

"I'll work from home for a few days," Samantha said. "My entire family is in California. It's the only time of year we're together, so it's a whole thing."

"I get that Christmas is a big deal, but that leaves us with only a couple weeks to nail down logistics."

I said I understood the hype around Christmas, but it didn't make sense to take off half the month of December for one holiday.

Do you really need that much vacation time?

There was a part of me that liked having the office to myself. I was way more productive without the noise, banter about the weekend, interruptions, and distractions of other people.

Last year, I nibbled on leftover holiday client gifts—Harry and David sweets, an Edible Arrangements fruit bouquet, good cheese, and roasted Virginia peanuts. I hosted a cocktail party of one. And the work got done. That's all I asked of Samantha, that we complete our work with excellence.

"We'll just use all the same documents and plans from the L.A. event as templates. Have the intern do the initial research. And you should be able to knock out these website changes quickly. Besides, they still have wi-fi on planes, right?" I asked with a chuckle. "You can get a lot done on a long flight."

"Of course." Samantha forced a smile so tight and wide, it had to hurt. "Oh, before I forget. Here's your gift. Merry Christmas."

She dropped it in a thud on my desk. I imagined it was a fruit-scented candle or maybe another mug with some inspirational saying scrawled across the front. The gift bag matched Samantha's atrocious sweater dress. Wooly and bright red, it featured every Christmas symbol imaginable. Santa's jolly, pink-cheeked face. Candy canes and gingerbread men. Golden lights ringed around her curvy frame. I believe I spotted the three wise men walking on her shoulder.

Samantha's get-up was part of the office's "Ugly Christmas Sweater Party." I had thrown on my usual costume of black pants, white button-down, and a gray cardigan. I planned to opt-out of all the 'fun' to meet Thin Quick's deadlines.

"Thanks for this." I made a mental note to ship out a card and gift to her, because she surely wasn't on my gift list. Truth be told I didn't even have a list.

"Do you need anything else before I'm out of the office?"

"I think that will be all. If I need anything, I'll send you a quick e-mail."

"Ebony, I'm not checking e-mail over Christmas. Everybody will be out of the office, including our client."

Was that a dig at the fact that I would likely be the only person toiling away with budget worksheets and tinkering with venue layouts instead of sipping eggnog and unwrapping gifts?

Before I could react, our receptionist Kim poked her head in.

"I'm so sorry to interrupt your meeting, but it's your sister. Again. She threatened to," Kim paused to look at the note she'd written, pushing her glasses to the tip of her nose. "In her words, 'come up here and get you her-doggone-self,' if I didn't put her through."

Like I said, drama queen.

"Sure, send the call through," I sighed, holding a finger up to Samantha. "This should only take a moment."

I picked up the phone before it finished the first ring.

"Alexis, what in the world is —"

"Manny's in the hospital." She dropped the news in a breathless cry. "He's in the emergency room right now. The ambulance came and picked him up. One minute he was up on the ladder, then the next—"

"Wait, what? Slow down." I rose and turned my back to Samantha, feeling more in control of the situation standing up. Besides, I didn't want anybody seeing the breakdown I felt coming on.

"...I don't know...maybe a heart attack, but I've been at the hospital for over an hour now, and they won't tell me nothing..."

Walls bearing framed pictures of client events across the world closed in on me. Normally, the expansive view of downtown Atlanta stirred a sense of bold confidence within, but now I felt light-headed. Like I was falling. Dark gray clouds gathered over the city. Over me. The sparkling clean glass reflected the visage of a fearful girl instead of my face. Coldness emanated from the thick window, but all I felt was heat, burning from my toes up.

Worry I hadn't met in a long time filled my eyes. I pressed the silver cross necklace against my lips, a wordless prayer ran through my mind. I wanted to yell for Alexis to stop talking, but I knew what this was like. I'd been here before.

"...I can't go through this by myself. You need to come home, Ebony. Just in case..."

My sister-in-law's frantic cries sounded eerily like the voices I'd heard deliver the worst news of my life 10 years ago. Alexis became a muffled sound far away, the steady pounding of my heart filling my ears.

A heart attack at his age? My brother isn't even 40 years old yet. God, this isn't fair.

As if it would hold me together, I hugged my chest, the silver and gold charms on my bracelet jingling. I couldn't stop shaking.

"Hey, is everything okay?" Samantha eked out, startling me from both past and present tragedies.

Warm tears streamed down my cheeks. I closed my eyes, not wanting to see that girl anymore. I wished I could shut out everybody and everything, especially the dire news about my brother.

"I have to go home."

Chapter Two

When I left Aurbor Grove 10 years ago, I swore I'd never return. I didn't want to revisit the tragic night that changed my life. I definitely didn't want to deal with the judgmental stares and whispers behind my back about what I did.

So far, I'd been able to keep that promise and create the perfect, new life. I worked very hard, being the best and giving my best so that I could get the best. When I was a little girl, dreaming up my future, my plan didn't look exactly like this, but I was close enough.

One sentence made me want to risk it all: "Manny's in the hospital."

My brother was all I had left in this world. The thought of life without him put everything in focus — all that other stuff became a blurry background, second tier, and meaningless in a minute. And I felt foolish for ever seeing it all differently.

The last time I saw Manny was six months ago. After plotting and planning for months, we found a date that worked with my hectic schedule. We met in Atlanta, catching up over cheese dip and crispy fried chicken tacos at my favorite lunch spot, Taqueria del Sol. For hours, we talked about everything from the Atlanta Falcons to the financial crisis.

Manny had grand plans—for his family and the business. He excitedly shared bold, audacious ideas about transforming the Aurbor Grove Inn into a destination for vacations, weddings, and special occasions. He wanted to take the small bed and breakfast our parents established to the next level. And based on the level of passion in his voice, I believed he would.

I remember thinking how proud they would be of him for carrying on their vision, then selfishly wondering what they'd think of me for abandoning it.

What if that was the last time I saw him?

I closed my eyes, inhaled deeply. Searching. Flipping through the memories of that day. The smile that stretched wide when he first saw me made me feel warm on the inside. But I couldn't remember what he wore or the sound of his voice.

Did I tell him I loved him?

I wanted to run out of the office, but I could not move. My personal, private life crashed head-on into my professional one, rendering me paralyzed.

"Ebony? Ebony, you're scaring me." Samantha's voice cut through the haze of emotions, thoughts, and memories.

"I-I have to go home." A quiet urgency filled my tone, but my pumps were rooted to the carpet.

Samantha gently took the phone from my hand, the dial tone blaring. "What happened? What's wrong?" she asked.

"My brother's in the hospital. He may have had a heart attack, or something? I don't know. My sister...she was hysterical. I have to go, now."

I stumbled toward my desk, gripping the edge. Taking a deep breath, I willed myself to get it together. I wanted, no, I needed to be strong – for myself, Manny, and Alexis. But that girl in the glass haunted me.

"Sit down for a moment."

Samantha guided me to my chair, her hands on my shoulders. She offered to take me home. And she wasn't talking about my condo down the street. She was willing to shift her plans to drive me *home-home* three hours away to Aurbor Grove.

She knew that I didn't drive. Technically, I could but chose not to get behind the wheel. Sometimes that was tough in a city like Atlanta, but I managed. Living downtown made it easier – everything I needed was a few blocks or a train stop away. Anyplace farther outside the perimeter, I relied on UBER or Lyft. Getting from Atlanta to Aurbor Grove during rush hour would prove to be trickier.

I sunk in my chair, staring out at the bumper-to-bumper traffic building on Peachtree Street. Beads of rain slid down the window, surely doubling commute times.

I need to go home.

The bright white Ferris wheel near Centennial Park turned slowly. Manny loved stuff like that—whether climbing to the tallest branch on a tree or hopping on the craziest ride at the amusement park. He always had to drag me along on his adventures.

"Give me your cell. I'll call your sister to let her know I'm bringing you home," Samantha said. I didn't fight it – the usual rebel inside gave up quite easily.

"Hi, yes, this is actually Ebony's coworker, Samantha..." she began, stepping a few feet away. A few minutes later, she handed my phone back to me.

"Alexis said she told you that she had sent someone to pick you up. Maybe you missed that part. I know it's a lot to take in." Samantha made a pained expression of pity, tucking a blond strand behind her studded ear. She had that mom voice on again, but it was warm and tender, and I needed that right now.

"I made sure she had the correct address, and I'll tell the security desk to send them straight up." Samantha glanced at her neon pink watch that also calculated every step and wink of sleep. "Your sister said your ride should arrive in a couple of hours, but I can wait with you. I don't mind skipping the party."

"No, no," I sniffled, waving her away. "You need to go. I will be fine. And I'm sure my brother will be fine too."

At least I hope so, I thought as Samantha hugged me goodbye.

* * *

As always, my boss Paula was last to leave the office.

She emphasized that as head of the firm—she was first in and last to leave. Having given the staff an early release for the Christmas party, she too departed much earlier.

"I feel so bad leaving you here alone." She balanced her purse and gift bags in her arms. Her sweater wasn't nearly as ugly as Samantha's. Dancing reindeer raised up their hooves over the words: Ready to Party.

"I promise I will be okay."

I hadn't cried in an hour. Crunching the numbers for a tight budget kept my mind so occupied, I didn't think about my brother lying in a hospital bed.

"I was able to catch up on the Thin Quick account," Paula said.

That sent my anxiety antenna straight up.

"The L.A. launch event drew our largest crowds and some of the best media coverage ever," she said. "The client sounds extremely satisfied. And it's certainly nice for us to get some extra budget before year-end."

"I couldn't have done it without Samantha and the rest of the team."

"Thanks to your leadership," she said. "Well, I have some gifts for you." She placed a shimmery, gold bag and another file atop all the others on my desk. The shiny, red Christmas bow stuck on the manila folder caught the glint of the fluorescent light hovering overhead.

Opening the folder to the offer letter for Vice President, my eyes widened. It outlined my new job description, duties, and management responsibilities.

Talk about a bittersweet day.

"It's not official until you sign off on the paperwork," she began, her voice dropping to a whisper, "and I hope you will."

My mouth hung open a little when my eyes ran across the salary increase, perks, and bonus. This job would push me into a new tax bracket.

I started spending the money – in my mind – immediately. I could upgrade my kitchen, get those shoes I'd been eyeing, take a real vacation...

"I want you to take the lead on all major corporate accounts for our Atlanta, New York, and D.C. offices."

"Oh my God," I muttered.

Have you ever wanted something so badly, that when you finally got it, you just didn't know how to act? I wanted to leap into her arms, but I clasped my hands together and held them against my lips.

"I cannot thank you enough."

"Don't thank me. You have given your very best on every single project," Paula said. "You'll have to hit the ground running, so get plenty of rest over the holidays. Take care of yourself and your family."

"We still have some things to—"

"Uh-uh. You're off the next week." She shook her head

and wagged a finger. "Today's your last day until *after* Christmas."

"I usually don't take Christmas off. Really, I don't mind working," I said.

"Ebony, when you move to this level, you have to know how to delegate. Your team can't grow if you don't give them the opportunity to take on more responsibilities."

"But, what if something goes wrong?"

Paula tossed her head back, laughing. "It probably will. Isn't Samantha your Account Director? Let her put out the fires. She has to learn how to run the account without you."

"Wait, you're taking the Thin Quick account away from me?"

"No, it will still be your account. But so will a dozen others, so managing your time is key," Paula said. "As a VP your job won't be to manage the day-to-day details, but people. You will still be the client's main point of contact, but you won't have to worry about the weeds anymore. Just maintain the forest."

But what if I liked the weeds? While excited about the promotion, it felt like Paula was ripping my baby from my arms. All I could think of were the worst-case scenarios happening on the Thin Quick account, and I wouldn't be there to fix things. Sure, I had capable colleagues, but sometimes they didn't do things the right way — my way.

Then it dawned on me, I'd never managed teams across multiple offices. I was moving up faster than most at my age. And the way Paula described the new role, it would be a huge transition from what I was most familiar with doing.

What if I wasn't ready for that level of management?

"Give Samantha the reigns on Thin Quick," Paula interrupted the internal mini-meltdown.

"No," I almost shouted. "I mean, I don't know if that's a

good idea. She's traveling home today, and I'd hate to drop everything on her."

"I'm sure she can manage from home. Isn't it pretty much the same tasks from the L.A. event? I'll also reach out to the New York office to get a team together that can help out too."

"But — "

"Let them take care of it. I'm serious. I better not get any e-mails from you. Not one. I need you fresh. Can you do that for me?" she asked, but didn't wait for an answer.

Once the frosted glass doors to our office suite closed behind Paula, I picked up my phone to call Manny and tell him my good news. His cell phone went straight to voicemail and when I heard his voice asking me to leave a message, I remembered where he was.

What if I never heard that voice again?

Nobody counseled or celebrated with me like my big brother. I could not imagine my life without Manny.

"God, please help me get through this," I whispered.

That was as much of a prayer I could bring myself to say. Truthfully, anger surged on the inside. None of this made sense to me. Our family had already gone through so much loss and pain, now my brother. There's only so much bending you can do before you break, right?

I dialed Manny's number just to hear him again.

* * *

The storm was long gone, and the city buildings at my back lit up as the sun drifted lower. By the time the sky went from fuchsia and orange watercolors to inky black, I'd finished the New York event proposal and started sketching out content ideas for the campaign website.

Since Paula wouldn't allow me to touch my account until after Christmas, I wanted to get as much done as possible.

The TV on full volume, a reporter warned that traffic was worse than usual because of the earlier surprise rain showers.

I wondered if whoever was coming to pick me up would get delayed. In the mix of emotions, I didn't think to ask Samantha for a name when she called Alexis to check on my ride.

Oh God, I hope it's not my cousin Gwen. She's going to talk me to death about people and places I don't know. But there was no way Gwen would volunteer to fight through Atlanta traffic. She refused to drive an hour outside of town.

I thumbed in a quick message to Alexis, asking about my ride.

...

The ellipsis letting me know that she was typing a response popped up on the phone screen, then disappeared. A few seconds later, the three dots within a conversation bubble appeared again.

Finally, her message came through.

Alexis: He will be there soon.

It shouldn't have taken her that long to tap out such a short answer. And it still didn't answer my question.

"But who is he?" I said aloud as I typed.

The dots played hide-and-go-seek on my screen alerting me that once again she was starting and stopping a message. It took her just as long to type an even shorter message this time.

One name.

My eyes bugged out, and the phone tumbled onto the carpet.

About the Author

Lakeshia Poole crafts compelling stories that spark change and connect people. As a writer, speaker and trainer, Lakeshia empowers and encourages a variety of audiences. She has brought the principles of *Faith Beats Fear* to life through events and discussions that guide people from worrier to warrior.

She previously published *Don't Let Me Fall*, *Exes and O's*, and *Happily Ever Christmas*. When she's not dreaming up new story ideas, Lakeshia is spending time with family or rooting for The University of Georgia Bulldogs.